The Broken Notes Saga

Book One

THE
FIRST
BROKEN

NOTE

Kristina Balla

First edition

ISBN: 979-8-9942653-1-4

For my kids-
and for everyone who stood beside
me while I learned to tell my own
story.

CONTENTS

INTRODUCTION

Before the music starts, before the lights rise, before the crowd becomes a living heartbeat—there's another world backstage. A hidden world. A world with its own rules, rhythms, and dangers.

It's a place I've lived in.
A place I know.
A place that has stayed with me long after the shows ended.

People see concerts as magic.
But behind that magic is a crew of people who work in the shadows—people who lift, build, rig, run, record, carry, patch, and protect. People who fix disasters before anyone ever notices. People who keep thousands safe every night.

And sometimes, despite everything they do... something still goes wrong.

This book was born from that reality.
From the late-night load-outs.
From the long bus rides between cities.
From the moments of humor that get you through exhaustion.
From the unspoken bond between crew members—family made by necessity, trust, and grit.
And from the quiet thought no one says aloud:

What if something went wrong on purpose?

The First Broken Note is fiction.
But the sweat, the pressure, the adrenaline, the chaos, and the love for the road—the heartbeat of live music—those parts are real.

This story is for:

-the crew who carry a show on their backs

-the artists who trust them

-the fans who feel the magic

-and the ones who stand in the shadows, making sure the music plays on

Riley Chase may be fictional, but she represents every person backstage who has ever seen something others missed... and stepped forward anyway.

Thank you for stepping into this world. Thank you for trusting me to guide you through it.

Now—

the house lights are fading.

It's time for the first broken note.

-Kristina Balla

CHAPTER ONE
The Fall

Kentucky mornings used to smell like damp earth and woodsmoke.
Or at least, that's how Riley Chase remembered them.

Memory was funny that way—selective, generous, willing to sand down the sharp edges if you let it.

She hadn't lived here in over two years—not since she'd packed everything she owned into a fading hatchback, left eastern Kentucky in the rearview, and moved to Nashville armed with nothing but a playlist of questionable confidence and the kind of ambition that made people worry quietly about her mental stability. She'd crossed the Kentucky border plenty since, but never long enough to let the air feel familiar.

Long enough to pass through. Never long enough to belong again.

Now, stepping off Crew Bus One into Lexington Arena's loading dock, familiarity hit her like a sucker punch.

Except Lexington Arena didn't smell like Kentucky mornings.

It smelled like metal grit, stale concession dust, and the ozone tang of too many amps warming up at once—a cocktail she privately classified as Load-In Number Five of the Tour.

The smell of a building waking up hungry.

It was barely seven a.m. The sun hadn't even started its shift. But the loading dock throbbed with motion: forklifts reversing with shrill beeps, road cases rumbling across concrete, riggers shouting measurements from the rafters, radios half-barking, half-panicking. Techs moved with the grim determination of people who had traded their circadian rhythms for paycheck stability.

This was the part fans never saw—the machinery before the magic, the noise before the music.

Riley stood in the middle of it, black jeans, black hoodie, hair shoved into a ponytail, laminate hooked to her beltloop thumping her hip every time she moved—trying not to look like the newest member of a massive machine. She'd worked tours before. But this was Jetstream. Twenty thousand seats. Machinery on a scale she'd only imagined until now.

A band big enough that momentum mattered more than people.

No pressure.

"KENTUCKY!"

Mara Valdez's voice cut through the noise like a snare crack.

Mara strode toward her wearing sunglasses indoors—pre-sunrise—because Mara respected neither natural light nor God's intended schedule. Underneath, her eyeliner looked sharp enough to commit crimes, and her walk suggested she fully intended to.

"There she is," Mara said, thrusting a roll of gaff tape into Riley's hand. "Quit sightseeing. Sleep is canceled. We've got a day."

Gaff tape: the unofficial currency of competence.

"Morning to you too," Riley said.

"It's not morning. It's pre-morning. A cursed time. Move."

They stepped through the tunnel and into the main bowl.

Empty seats stretched into the dark in every direction, waiting for twenty thousand screaming fans tonight. For now, though, the place felt like a sleeping giant.

Big rooms always felt like this before load-in—quiet, patient, dangerous if you underestimated them.

The stage was in pieces—riser frames, cable coils, motor points dangling from the grid like metallic stalactites. High above, riggers in harnesses traversed the catwalk with steady, confident steps that made Riley's stomach lurch.

Gravity didn't care how experienced you were.

Every venue had its personality.

Lexington's felt... alert.

Probably just being home again.
Probably just nerves.

Probably nothing worth naming.

Mara snapped her fingers. "Map me."

Riley pointed as they walked. "Dressing rooms down that hall. Guest rooms opposite. Catering near the freight elevator. VIP through that vom. And if anyone touches that tunnel, they die. That's where we stash carts."

Logistics were power. Knowing where things lived meant knowing who controlled them.

Mara squinted. "Look at Kentucky showing off."

"I fake competence well."

"Same," Mara said, "but with charisma."

They moved through the usual pre-show ritual: checking cable runs, seam lines, deck edges, trip hazards, power drops. Mara narrated with the chaotic confidence of someone who believed sarcasm counted as cardio.

Riley glanced up at the grid. A rigger leaned to adjust a point.

Her ribs buzzed.

A strange, low hum beneath bone.

Not painful.

Not familiar.

Like standing too close to a live wire without touching it.

She pressed a hand to her sternum.

"You good?" Mara asked.

"Yeah. Just—home weird," Riley said.

"Ah, emotional damage. Classic."

A forklift zipped past at a speed that absolutely violated OSHA and common sense. Riley flinched.

"Relax," Mara said. "Sound guys aren't awake yet. You're safe."

Famous last words on any tour.

"Comforting."

"Don't get used to it."

They walked into a patch of open floor beneath the center grid.

Her ribs buzzed again.

Not nerves.

Not déjà vu.

Something quieter. More deliberate.

Like the building noticed her.

Like it was taking inventory.

She shook it off.

"Alright," Mara said, "we've got—"

A shout ripped from the rafters.

"HEY—NO—STOP—STOP—!"

Riley's head snapped up.

A rigger halfway across the grid struggled—his descender jammed, his foot slipping off the beam. His harness jerked sideways in a way no harness should.

A mistake had already been made. She could feel it.

Time split open.

Mara yelled something—maybe "MOVE!"—but it drowned under the thunder in Riley's ears.

The safety line whipped.

The rigger fell.

Straight down.

A sixty-foot freefall

A full drop.

No bounce. No second chance.

Riley didn't think—there wasn't time to.

Mara slammed into her, shoving her out of the fall zone.

A sickening THUD cracked through the bowl.

Radios erupted. Someone screamed. Someone swore. Someone threw up behind a case.

The machine didn't stop. It just absorbed the noise.

Riley pushed to her elbows, dizzy.

Her ribs weren't buzzing now.

They were shrieking.

And then she saw it—

A glint on the concrete.

Right where her knee had been a moment earlier.

A charm.

Small. Silver. Shaped like a music note.

Perfect. Clean.

Not fallen.

Placed.

Too deliberate to belong to chaos.

Her heart stuttered.

"Riley—don't—" Mara snapped, but Riley already lifted it.

The charm was warm.

Not floor warm.

Held warm.

As if it had been waiting.

A faint vibration pulsed in her palm.

Her ribs answered like an echo.

This wasn't dropped.

This wasn't random.

"...No way that's an accident," she whispered.

"No," Mara said quietly. "It's not."

And suddenly the arena didn't feel like home.

It felt occupied.

They retreated into a tunnel hallway, away from the chaos. Riley leaned against cold concrete, trying to breathe evenly.

Cold helped. Cold made things real.

"You did good," Mara said gently.

Riley let out a humorless laugh. "I watched someone die and picked up evidence. That's not 'good.'"

"You didn't scream," Mara said. "You didn't bolt. You didn't get in the way. That's tour-good."

"Tour-good is a low bar."

"You say that like most people don't trip over it."

9

Riley slid a hand into her pocket. The charm was still warm. Still pulsing.

Like it hadn't finished saying what it came to say.

"Mara," she whispered. "Have you ever seen something like this? A fall like that?"

Mara's expression tightened. "Once. Different tour. Different city. Same sick feeling."

"Was it equipment failure?"

Mara hesitated.

"They called it that," she said. "Insurance paperwork taller than you."

"But was it?"

A beat passed.

"That's the thing about touring," Mara said quietly. "By the time anybody finds the truth, the show's moved on to the next city."

Truth didn't travel well. Tours did.

The charm pulsed again.

Her ribs agreed.

Riley shivered.

"Look at me," Mara said, bumping her shoulder. Riley did. "Right now your job is to breathe, drink water, and not faint in front of Sloan. Got it?"

"Got it," Riley whispered.

"Good. Because here's the fun part: we still have to set up dressing rooms."

Riley blinked. "We're still doing the show?"

"If Sloan has any say?" Mara snorted. "Unless the building is literally on fire by doors, she'll run it."

Riley thought of the rigger. "But someone just—"

"Show must go on," Mara said. "Oldest lie in the business. Come on. Before the band shows up and sees you looking like a ghost who saw a different ghost."

Or worse—a liability.

Riley pushed off the wall.

The hallway lights flickered.

Just a glitch.

Just old infrastructure.

Probably.

Her ribs buzzed once.

She ignored it.

They snagged a cart stacked with supplies and pushed it toward the band's dressing-room hallway.

"Okay," Mara said, in fake-peppy mode. "Deep breath. Time to turn this murder castle into a four-star hotel."

"This is deeply unhealthy coping," Riley muttered.

"Tour life, baby."

They reached the headliner's dressing-room door. A black paper sign with the band's logo—white jagged letters—had been taped crookedly to it.

Mara straightened the sign automatically. "Grab the humidifier. I'll do lighting first."

They moved in practiced rhythm.

Riley unboxed the humidifier and set it near the corner. Filled it with water, plugged it into a power strip that already hosted three other devices, frowned, then moved the strip to a safer-looking outlet.

Mara adjusted lamp placement, swapping out harsh overheads for soft lamps. The room shifted from interrogation-chic to moody lounge with a few clicks.

"Plants," Mara said.

"On it," Riley replied.

They arranged three fake potted plants on the coffee table and side surfaces. The effect was... almost convincing.

Riley stepped back, arms crossed.

"Look at us," she said. "Aesthetic geniuses."

"Don't get cocky," Mara said. "We still have to color-sort the snacks."

Riley groaned. "You're kidding."

"Do I look like I'm kidding?"

"Yes."

"Well I'm not. The band's gone through every phase of tour superstition. Last run, they had to do a pre-show circle in the same order every night. This run, the M&M's have to be rainbowed. I don't write the rules. I just suffer under them."

Riley opened the snack crate and began sorting small packets of candies and chips into vague color schemes.

Mara watched her for a beat.

"You sure you're okay?" she asked again, quieter this time.

"Define okay."

"Not about to cry or black out," Mara said. "That's my working standard."

Riley hesitated.

The image of the fall flashed behind her eyes—

the harness, the slip, the brutal stop.

Her stomach rolled.

But something else popped up too.

A flicker of memory.

Her dad's voice, years ago, sitting at their tiny kitchen table in eastern Kentucky, hands stained with grease from his day job, telling her stories about "the road."

Not the romantic version.

The real one.

"Rule number one, bug," he'd said with a half-smile. "You respect gravity. Everyone thinks sound and light are the dangerous parts. They're not. It's what's over your head that gets you."

She'd laughed it off at twelve.

It didn't feel funny now.

"I'm... not okay," she admitted. "But I'm here."

Mara nodded once. "That counts."

Riley dropped a bag of yellow candies into the "gold" bowl.

"Do accidents like this... ever feel like more than accidents?" she asked.

Mara's jaw worked.

"Sometimes," she said carefully. "Sometimes it feels like a bunch of little mistakes gang up on the wrong person. And sometimes..." She trailed off.

"Sometimes?" Riley pushed.

"Sometimes it feels like something else," Mara said. "But if you start thinking every bad thing is a pattern, you'll lose your mind."

Riley thought of the charm again.

"Yeah," she said softly. "Right."

There was a knock at the dressing-room door.

Mara tensed. "If that's the drummer wanting to 'rearrange the energy,' I'm jumping out a window."

Riley opened the door.

It wasn't the drummer.

It was Theo.

He stood there in jeans and a dark hoodie, curls a little damp like he'd showered and hadn't bothered to dry them properly. His guitar case hung from one shoulder, strap worn but loved.

Up close, he looked both taller and more... human than he did under stage lights.

Less untouchable.

More real.

His gaze flicked over the room quickly—humidifier, plants, lamps, snack bowls.

Then it landed on her.

"You okay?" he asked quietly.

She opened her mouth.

Found herself saying: "Yeah. I'm fine."

Liar.

Theo's brow furrowed. He didn't buy it.

"I heard there was a fall," he said. "They're saying it was... bad."

"It was," she said.

He studied her face for a long moment.

Behind them, Mara cleared her throat dramatically. "Starboy, you're not supposed to see the room before it's perfect. It ruins the illusion."

Theo's mouth twitched. "Morning, Mara."

"It was," she said. "Now it's deeply concerning."

He ignored her and stepped a little closer to Riley, lowering his voice.

"If you need to sit down, or get air, or not be here for soundcheck," he said, "you can. Sloan won't like it, but she'll live. I know what it's like for a fall to stick in your head."

Riley blinked. "You do?"

"First tour I ever did," he said quietly, "a light tech fell off a ladder during changeover. He was okay. Broken arm. But for days I couldn't look up at the rig without feeling like the world was tilting."

That was... more than she expected him to say.

The Theo she'd seen in interviews was quiet, guarded, half-smiling. On stage he was a different creature entirely, caught up in the music, but offstage he'd mostly slid through spaces like a shadow so far.

This Theo, right now, offering her a piece of his first-tour trauma?

That felt big.

Her chest squeezed—not the weird buzzing, just something human and soft.

"Thanks," she said. "I'll be okay. I think."

He nodded slowly. "If you're lying, at least lie to someone less observant."

Mara made a choking sound. "Wow. Flirting and emotional awareness. They grow up so fast."

Theo colored slightly. "I'm not—this is not—"

Riley surprised herself by laughing. It came out shaky, but real.

Mara looked satisfied. "There. She laughed. Good job. You may stay."

Theo shrugged the guitar case higher on his shoulder. "Show must go on, right?"

Mara and Riley shared a look.

Riley answered.

"Or," she said, "we pretend it does."

Theo's eyes met hers, and something passed between them:

An understanding that the day had cracked.

And no one was going to admit how deep.

He nodded once more and stepped back into the hall.

"I'll see you later," he said. "If you feel weird, come find me."

She raised an eyebrow. "Is that medical advice?"

"It's... advice-adjacent."

The corner of his mouth lifted.

Then he was gone, disappearing into the maze of backstage corridors.

Mara watched Riley watching him leave.

"Oh," she said thoughtfully. "You're in trouble."

Riley turned. "What?"

Mara pointed at her. "You have 'trauma-bond crush' written all over you. Very messy. Ten out of ten, will generate chaos."

Riley rolled her eyes, but her cheeks warmed. The charm pulsed.

Her ribs buzzed back.

Someone knew she had picked it up.

Someone who had placed it.

Someone still here.

Watching.

CHAPTER TWO
Statements

Backstage should have roared back to life.

Load-ins usually snapped back fast—even after injuries, even after emergencies.

But this time?

Silence clung to the air like fog.

The kind that didn't lift when the sun came up—because it wasn't weather. It was aftermath.

Crew members clustered in uneasy groups, talking in whispers, as if no one wanted to speak louder than the sound of the rigger hitting the floor.

Grief didn't have a radio channel. It just seeped into everything.

Riley stayed close to Mara, one hand gripping her clipboard, the other curled tightly around the charm in her pocket. The metal dug into her palm—warm, present, impossible to ignore.

She kept expecting it to change shape. To bite. To turn into a joke with teeth.

Her ribs buzzed again.

A low, steady thrum.

Like her bones remembered something her brain didn't want to.

Like the inside of her chest had become a tuning fork and someone had struck it.

"Deep breaths, Kentucky," Mara murmured. "You look like someone shoved you into a freezer."

Riley exhaled shakily. "I'm trying."

"Try harder," Mara said, though the bite softened. She nudged Riley's elbow. "And stop touching your pocket. Sloan's on high alert. She'll sniff out secrets like a bloodhound who's tired of everyone's bullshit."

"I wasn't—"

"You were," Mara deadpanned. "You've got pocket-hovering energy."

If anxiety were visible, Riley would be wearing it like a reflective vest.

Riley dropped her hand—but the charm felt heavier, like it knew it wasn't supposed to be found.

21

Like it knew it belonged to someone else.

Whatever it was, it wasn't random. And her ribs agreed.

They rounded the corner toward the production office... and found Sloan waiting dead center of the hallway.

Arms crossed.
Jaw clenched to shattering.
Clipboard hugged to her chest like she was bracing for impact.

Sloan's clipboard was a weapon, a shield, and occasionally a court summons.

Her sleek ponytail, normally precise, had broken strands sticking out near her temple.

She did not look like a woman in control of a multimillion-dollar show.
She looked scared.

Sloan never looked scared. Sloan looked like she'd bite a bear and win. This was different.

Two uniformed officers stood by the door. A plainclothes detective pulled on latex gloves—sharp eyes, calm posture, the kind of woman who could walk into chaos and take its pulse.

Detective Ruiz.

Riley recognized her from safety briefings and crew rumors. Ruiz was the kind of investigator whose gaze alone made people rethink their life choices.

The kind of woman who didn't raise her voice because she didn't have to.

And right now, she was looking directly at Riley.

"Riley Chase?" Ruiz asked.

Riley froze. "Y-yes."

"I need your statement," Ruiz said. "You and Mara were closest to the fall. Both of you—come with me."

Ruiz didn't ask. She didn't need to. The air rearranged itself around her authority.

Sloan stepped forward like a fuse catching. "Detective, before you do anything, my crew is shaken, I have a band arriving in an hour, we still don't know the extent—"

Ruiz lifted a hand.

"Sloan. I know you've got a show to build." Her voice stayed calm, firm. "But a man died. I need Riley for fifteen minutes. You can spare her."

Sloan looked like she wanted to argue on principle, then remembered there were certain principles even she didn't bulldoze.

Sloan exhaled sharply. "Fine. Fifteen. Mara, go with her."

Mara saluted. "Aye aye, captain."

Ruiz guided them into a small lounge room—one of those multipurpose backstage spaces with mismatched chairs, a folding table, and half-empty water jugs stacked like offerings to the chaos gods.

Rooms like this existed in every venue. They were where you cried, negotiated, got fired, got promoted, and pretended you weren't terrified.

Riley's heartbeat felt wrong. Too high. Too fast. Too loud.

She kept her hand near her pocket, chest tight.

That charm wasn't just an object.
It felt like a message.
Like something had reached out and touched her.

Like someone had tapped her on the shoulder from the dark and then walked away smiling.

Ruiz gestured to the chairs. "Have a seat."

Mara dropped into her chair with all the protective big-sister energy of a guard dog. Riley sat beside her, spine stiff.

Ruiz clicked on a small recorder.

The red light blinked to life—tiny, unforgiving. Evidence had a heartbeat too.

"Riley Chase," she said evenly. "Tell me what you saw."

Riley didn't breathe in.
She counted instead.
One heartbeat. Two. Three.

The room waited with her, like it expected her to break first.

The memory came in sharp, brutal flashes:

The rigger's scramble.
The sudden twist of his harness.
The sickening drop.
The final, awful quiet.

She told Ruiz everything—
everything except the charm.

Not because she meant to lie.
Because every time she tried to speak the words, her ribs buzzed hard—an electric warning under her skin, as if something deep in her bones said don't.
Her throat locked.
Her tongue refused.

Like her body had made a decision without consulting her.

The charm throbbed faintly in her pocket, like a pulse answering her own.

She stumbled, regrouped, and continued the story without it.

Ruiz noticed.

Ruiz noticed everything. That was the point of her.

She didn't interrupt.
Didn't push.
But she saw it.

When Riley finished, Ruiz clicked her pen once.

"You hesitated," she said softly.

Riley swallowed. "I... didn't know what details mattered."

"Any detail matters," Ruiz said. "Even the strange ones. Even the small ones."

Especially the small ones. Big problems started there.

Riley felt the words like a weight. "I understand," she whispered.

Ruiz flipped to a new page.

"Did you see anyone in the rigging area beforehand? Anyone out of place?"

Riley shook her head. "No."

Ruiz watched her face carefully, then nodded.

"Alright. Next question: have you ever been involved in an incident like this before? On any tour?"

Something in Riley's mind flinched.

An old accident.

Back home.

Blood on concrete.

Sirens.

And a man telling her, years ago, to stop asking questions like questions were gasoline.

She forced a breath. "I—no. Not like this."

Ruiz didn't press.

She simply turned another page.

"The initial report says the primary descender jammed. But secondary lines should've prevented a fatal fall." Ruiz paused. "Unless someone tampered with it."

Riley's breath hitched.

The charm seemed to go still, listening.

Mara muttered, "Fantastic. Because gravity wasn't dangerous enough on its own."

Ruiz tapped her pen once more. "This stays internal until we know more. Riley—if anything else stands out to you, no matter how odd or irrelevant—call me immediately."

She slid a card across the table.

Riley didn't reach for it.

Her fingers wouldn't move.

Her hand felt like it belonged to somebody else. Somebody quieter. Somebody controlled.

Mara grabbed it for her and slipped it into her own pocket.

Ruiz stood. "We'll talk again soon."

The door shut behind her with a soft, definitive thud.

The silence that followed felt louder than the fall.

Like the building itself had leaned in.

The charm in Riley's pocket throbbed like a heartbeat.

Mara exhaled. "You good?"

"No," Riley said honestly. "Are you?"

"Oh, hell no." Mara stood. "But we're faking it until the band shows up, so let's go

---

They stepped back into the hallway—

And the air shifted.

Not the charm.

Not the rib-buzz.

Something else.

The kind of shift you felt when you stepped into a room mid-argument. When the temperature told you you'd missed a sentence that mattered.

Riley stopped.

Slowly turned.

A figure stood at the far end of the corridor.

Shadowed.

Still.

One hand resting lightly on the handle of a

rolling amp rack—too still, too poised, like someone waiting for her to notice.

Not startled. Not lost. Not in a hurry. That was what made it wrong.

As her eyes adjusted, the figure slipped behind the equipment and vanished.

Her blood iced.

"Problem?" Mara asked.

"I saw someone."

"This place is crawling with someones."

"No," Riley whispered. "Someone... watching."

Mara studied her face long enough to know this wasn't theatrics.

Mara's humor was armor, but she wasn't stupid. She'd survived too many docks to doubt a real warning.

Then she looped an arm through Riley's and tugged. "Come on, Kentucky. Paranoia's kicking in early. We're going to catering before you start seeing ghosts in the rafters."

Riley followed.

But she kept looking back.

Whoever had been standing there—

They weren't crew.

Weren't band.

Weren't venue.

Weren't cops.

They were something else.

Something that had been here long before she arrived.

And something that knew exactly where she was standing.

Catering smelled like bacon, scrambled eggs, and collective trauma.

It always smelled like that on show days. Today it just felt... honest.

Riley pushed her eggs around her plate. Mara inhaled pancakes with the focus of an Olympic event. Crew drifted in and out, quieter than usual, moving like they were afraid of waking the building up.

Theo walked in with Rowan. His expression was tight—until he spotted Riley. Then, just barely, his shoulders lowered.

The room didn't change when he entered. It just... noticed him. The way people did.

He hesitated near her table before approaching.

"You holding up?" he asked.

Riley opened her mouth to lie—

but her ribs buzzed sharply, like a correction.

"No," she said honestly. "Not really."

Theo nodded, slow and understanding. He crouched slightly to her level.

"I talked to Sloan," he said. "She's pretending everything's fine, which means nothing is fine."

"That tracks," Mara said through a mouthful of coffee.

"If you need to step away," Theo told Riley, "Even just for a minute, I've got you."

Not flirtatious. Not performative. Just... steady. Which somehow felt more dangerous.

"If I leave, I'll think about it more."

"Yeah," Theo said quietly. "I know that feeling."

He stood. "If you need anything— anything—come find me."

As he walked away, Mara raised an eyebrow. "Uh-huh. Trouble. Capital T. That boy is already planning wedding hashtags."

"Mara—"

"You sweet Appalachian cinnamon roll," Mara sighed. "You are so in danger."

But Riley barely heard her.

Because her ribs buzzed again—

longer this time.

Deliberate.

Like a finger drawing a line down her spine: pay attention.

She touched the charm in her pocket.

Cold now.

Too cold.

As if it had finally remembered what it was.

And she knew—without knowing how—that Detective Ruiz wasn't the only one who wanted her statement.

Someone else wanted to talk.

Someone who had been waiting

a very

long

time.

And backstage, waiting was an art.

CHAPTER THREE
Near Miss

Load-out in Lexington should have been predictable. Muscle memory. A practiced dance of wheels, straps, chains, and swearing.
It wasn't.

Predictable was a luxury tour life rarely allowed—but tonight, even the chaos felt wrong.

The fall had turned every crew member jittery. People checked their harnesses twice. Then a third time. Riggers descended from the grid with their shoulders tight, eyes scanning for problems that weren't there. Sound techs flinched at clinking metal. Lighting techs walked under the truss like it was a loaded weapon.

No one joked about gravity anymore.

Riley wasn't doing much better.

Her ribs buzzed at irregular intervals, each pulse a reminder of what she didn't understand. The charm in her pocket burned a little warmer than it should have.

And she kept catching glimpses of movement in her peripheral vision—shadows that dissolved whenever she spun to face them.

Tour fatigue could make you paranoid. So could adrenaline. So could knowing—deep down—that you weren't imagining it.

Mara walked beside her, keeping step, using sarcasm like duct tape.

"Relax," Mara said, hauling a cable cart behind them. "The odds of gravity committing two murders in one day are low."

"You're not helping," Riley muttered.

"I can do helpful. I just choose not to."

It was the closest Mara ever got to saying she was scared too.

Riley almost laughed.
Almost.

Then her ribs buzzed again, and the laughter died in her throat.

Sloan found them near the loading dock, under work lights that didn't flatter anyone. She was mid-argument with a union steward, voice sharp enough to cut stage curtains.

"No one touches the grid until Ruiz signs off," Sloan snapped. "No one. If anyone ignores that, I will personally superglue your boots to a forklift."

No one laughed. That was how you knew she meant it.

The steward backed off. Sloan turned toward Riley and Mara, her expression still blistering.

"Chase. Valdez. With me."

They followed her into a cramped production office where Detective Ruiz leaned against a folding table, reviewing a tablet with slow, deliberate taps.

Ruiz had the posture of someone who never rushed—and therefore never missed anything.

Ruiz looked up.

"I have questions."

Riley's stomach dropped. "About the fall?"

"About everything."

Sloan crossed her arms. "This isn't a formal interrogation, detective."

Ruiz ignored her.

She looked at Riley.

"Your statement was... thorough. Except for one detail."

Riley froze.

Her ribs buzzed.

Harder this time. Louder. Like a warning siren buried under skin.

Mara's eyes flicked toward Riley's pocket.

"The moment you approached the body," Ruiz said quietly, "you saw something."

Riley swallowed. "I—"

Ruiz waited.

Held the silence like a net.

It was a practiced stillness. The kind that made people confess just to fill the space.

Finally, Riley reached into her hoodie and withdrew the charm.

Ruiz's expression didn't change, but something behind her eyes sharpened.

"A music note," she murmured. "Interesting."

"I didn't want to touch it," Riley said quickly. "But I couldn't not. It felt—" She stopped, embarrassed. "—important."

Saying it out loud made it sound ridiculous. It hadn't felt ridiculous at the time.

Ruiz lifted it with gloved fingers, turning it under the light.

"This wasn't the rigger's," she said. "Not part of his gear. Not something that would fall from the grid." She paused. "Where was it?"

"Right beside him," Riley whispered.

"Placed," Ruiz said. Not a question. "Not dropped. Placed."

The word landed heavier than the charm itself.

Sloan swore under her breath.

Mara asked the question Riley couldn't make her mouth form.

"Detective... you think someone caused this?"

Ruiz didn't look up. "I think someone wanted you to find that charm."

Riley's skin prickled.

Her ribs buzzed again—faint, like agreement.

Like something inside her had just been acknowledged.

Ruiz bagged the charm and sealed it.

"I'm looping in other departments," Ruiz said. "There have been... incidents. Over the years. Accidents that don't behave like accidents."

"On other tours?" Mara asked.

Ruiz nodded once.

Riley felt the world tilt.

She thought of how many arenas she'd walked into without thinking twice. How many ceilings she'd trusted.

"Why us?" she whispered.

Ruiz's eyes met hers.

"Patterns pick people," she said. "Not the other way around."

And once a pattern noticed you, it didn't look away.

The words slid down Riley's spine like ice water.

Load-out dragged until nearly 2 a.m. The final truck closed with a clanging echo.

Sloan dismissed the crew, trying—badly—to hide her exhaustion.

Even control freaks hit their limits. They just collapsed later.

Riley walked toward the buses with Mara and Taj, the band's head of security, who never spoke unless something was already wrong. The night air was cold enough to bite. She pulled her sleeves over her hands, crumpling the cuffs into her palms like stress balls, tighter than she meant to.

"You're pale," Taj observed. "Paler than usual. That's saying something."

"Thanks," Riley muttered.

"No problem," Taj said. "I'm generous."

They reached the line of idling buses. Exhaust hung low and heavy in the air.

Engines hummed like animals waiting to be let loose.

Riley stopped at the steps to Crew Bus One, hand hovering over the railing. Something in her ribs pulsed—not pain. Not warning.

Persistence.

Like a finger tapping a table, waiting for her to look up.

She turned.

Someone was watching her.

She couldn't see them—not fully—but the sensation was unmistakable. A presence in the dark. A weight of attention.

Her skin crawled.

Whoever it was didn't rush. Didn't hide fast. They knew time was on their side.

Then Mara grabbed her elbow. "Hey. Don't ghost out. You're sleeping."

"I'm fine," Riley said.

"You're lying," Mara said. "You lie worse when you're tired."

Taj stood at the bottom of the bus steps, arms crossed. "You good getting on?"

Riley hesitated.

That alone answered him.

Taj's expression shifted—a rare seriousness. "Stay alert tonight. Keep your radio on channel four. I mean it."

Taj didn't do vague warnings. That was what scared her most.

Riley swallowed, nodded, climbed into the bus.

The bus was dark, the engine's hum steady beneath everything else.

Bunks lined both walls, private only by courtesy.

Exhaustion wrapped around her like something familiar.

She slid into her bunk, leaving the curtain half-open.

Her ribs buzzed once.

A slow vibration.

A reminder.

A promise.

This wasn't fear anymore. It was recognition.

She closed her eyes and tried to breathe.

But she knew.

The fall was only the beginning.

The charm was not an accident.

And someone, somewhere in the dark...

Knew who she was.

CHAPTER FOUR
Petty Crimes

They rolled into Cincinnati at 4:32 a.m. Crew Bus One hissed like it was disappointed to still be functioning.

The suspension groaned like it had opinions. Riley respected that.

Riley, who had slept approximately forty minutes and regretted every one of them, blinked awake to Mara shaking her shoulder like she was trying to restart a dead lawn mower.

"Up," Mara commanded. "Rise and resent."

Riley buried her face into her pillow. "No."

"Yes," Mara said, yanking the curtain open. "The sun isn't up either but we don't judge her. Equality."

Riley considered mutiny. Or death. Either felt reasonable.

They shuffled off the bus behind the other morning crew—an army of black hoodies, steel-toed boots, and people powered entirely by caffeine and spite.

Cincinnati watched them arrive without enthusiasm.

The Cincinnati arena loading dock hit Riley in the face like a crime.
It smelled like old popcorn, wet socks, and the emotional damage of a minor league hockey team.

"That can't be legal," Mara said, wrinkling her entire soul. "Whatever that is? Biohazard."

"Welcome to Ohio," Riley said. "They put cinnamon in chili. Laws are interpretive."

Mara stopped walking. "You're still lying about that."

"In the year of our Lord and Live Nation?" Riley said. "I wish I were."

"That's not cuisine," Mara insisted. "That's a municipal cry for help."

Somewhere, a city council member felt seen.

They joined the morning circus— forklifts beeping threats, riggers yelling distances, road cases stampeding like metallic buffalo. Radios barked nonsense. Someone shouted "WHO MOVED MY MULTI-TOOL?!" like it was an existential wound.

Touring grief looked a lot like routine— until it didn't.

Riley's ribs didn't buzz.

First time since Lexington.

She didn't trust it.

Quiet meant the storm was taking notes.

They walked the loop: tunnels, loading bays, dressing rooms, production, catering.

Riley clocked every exit without meaning to. Old habit. New instinct.

Every venue had its own flavor. This one felt like someone had designed it while actively hating people.

Low ceilings. No clear signage. One hallway that looped back on itself like an Ikea joke.

"Ambience," Mara declared. "Eau de Dumpster."

Somewhere, a fire marshal was crying.

They grabbed their ritual supplies cart—lamps, plants, humidifiers, towels, snacks—and headed for dressing rooms.

"You take band main," Mara said, cracking her neck like a prizefighter. "I'll do support. Make it smell less like mortality."

"Excellent," Riley said. "Love a challenge."

She didn't mention the faint sense that the building was listening.

The dressing room was barren: white walls, buzzing fluorescents, folding tables, a couch that had seen at least four divorces.

Probably two of them musical.

Riley got to work.

Lamps first, killing the interrogation-room vibe. Plants next—now three fake and one real, because Drew talked to them and no one had the heart to tell him they were plastic. Humidifier in the corner, humming to life like a tiny steam engine trying its best.

Riley adjusted the airflow twice. She didn't know why. She just needed it right.

On the coffee table she laid out snacks: chips, protein bars, chocolate, gummy vitamins some manager had sworn were essential. She added a bowl of individually wrapped candy for Asher, who stress-ate sugar like it paid him.

She flipped off the overheads. The room shifted from morgue to moody clubhouse in about thirty seconds.

Mara appeared in the doorway with an armful of black towels.

"Look at you," she said. "Saint of Vibes."

"We take our redemption where we can," Riley said.

"How's the ribcage?"

"Quiet."

Mara narrowed her eyes. "Quiet-quiet? Or horror movie quiet?"

"The second one."

"Fantastic," Mara said brightly. "Thriving."

Nobody mentioned the charm. Nobody mentioned Lexington. Silence was its own superstition.

Nobody said Lexington's name aloud. Nobody had to. You could feel it in the crew walk, the glances upward, the way Sloan now stared at rigging like she was trying to break its spirit.

Riley still felt the imprint of the charm in her palm.

"Catering?" Mara asked. "Let's go commit carb-related sins."

"In Ohio?" Riley said. "Those might be felonies."

"Even better," Mara replied.

Catering smelled like desperation and overcooked scrambled eggs. Long buffet tables sagged under lukewarm offerings. A staffer stirred something ominous in a steam tray.

Riley clocked the exits. Again.

Mara approached cautiously. "What is that?"

"Don't ask if you don't want chili," Riley said.

The staffer perked up. "Cincinnati-style! Chili over spaghetti!"

Mara stared like the woman had just confessed to arson.

"You... put soup on noodles."

"It's not soup," Riley said.

"It has cinnamon," Mara said sniffing and recoiling. "It's dessert-spaghetti. That's wrong in at least ten states."

Riley lifted her hands. "Ohio is a lawless frontier."

Somewhere, a fan would post a TikTok defending it with their whole chest.

A few crew members snorted. Humor was a survival mechanism.

Theo entered with Rowan and Asher—feral, pretty, unreasonably awake.

They always looked like that: half-rockstar, half-feral raccoon.

His eyes found Riley immediately.

He raised a brow.

You good?

Riley shrugged.

Define good.

His mouth twitched like he wanted to argue that point.

Mara elbowed her. "Stop flirting with your eyebrows."

49

"I'm not—"

"She is," Asher chimed in. "Let her live."

"Eat your cursed spaghetti," Mara said.

They sat. Riley attempted a plain bagel. Mara autopsied her plate.

"If I die from this chili," Mara declared, "tell my family I died doing what I loved."

"Complaining?" Riley asked.

"Correct."

Riley lifted her coffee.

Her ribs buzzed.

Soft.

Insistent.

Like a fingertip tapping glass.

She froze.

Mara noticed instantly. "What?"

Riley's attention pulled—slow, magnetic—to the water cooler.

She didn't smell anything wrong. Didn't see anything wrong. She just knew.

"I don't think anyone should drink that," she whispered.

Mara didn't hesitate. "HEY! NOBODY TOUCH THE COOLER!"

Mara never waited for proof. She trusted Riley's instincts the way some people trusted religion.

A lighting tech frowned. "Why?"

Riley moved closer—

her ribs buzzing harder with each step.

Then she saw it:

A puncture near the base.

Plastic tubing wedged downward.

Sabotage.

"Is that supposed to be there?" she asked the staffer.

The staffer went white. "No. No, absolutely not."

Theo approached. "Riley?"

"Someone modified the jug," she whispered.

The word *someone* felt heavier every time she said it.

Before Mara could unleash holy hell, Sloan and Detective Ruiz strode in like mirrored storms.

Ruiz crouched. "Backflow valve."

Sloan cursed loud enough to scare a table of sound guys.

Ruiz turned to Riley. "How did you notice?"

"I just... felt it."

Ruiz didn't question the logic.

She logged it.

Which was worse.

As Ruiz sealed the evidence bag, Riley caught the faint outline etched into the plastic housing behind the valve – a broken note, small and deliberate, like a signature left where no one was meant to look.

Soundcheck should have been smooth. It wasn't.

It never was after something went wrong.

Half the arena was dark, seats yawning into the half-light. Fans clustered in VIP pit, buzzing with teen excitement and poor spelling on signs.

Jax waved. Rowan cracked knuckles. Asher winked at somebody's grandmother.

The crowd screamed like nothing bad had ever happened backstage. They never knew.

Theo stepped to his mark, slid in his in-ears, glanced toward Riley.

Check-in.

Connection.

Grounding.

He did that more now.

Music started.

Lights flickered.

Wrong cues. Wrong colors. Wrong timing.

Riley lifted her radio. "Sloan, we're getting unprogrammed—"

A voice slid into her comm.

Not Sloan.

Not Mara.

Not anyone with clearance.

Calm.

Measured.

Intentional.

"Riley."

Her lungs forgot their job.

Her ribs didn't buzz. They *locked*.

She scanned the floor. The tunnels. The catwalk.

"Stay still," the voice murmured. "I wanted to see if you could hear me over the music."

Her ribs went electric.

"Who are you?" she whispered.

"You're in a box," he said. "Little lights. Little stage. Little gate. Easy to bend."

The arena suddenly felt very small.

Her mouth went dry.

"Leave the tour," he said. "And your thread ends. Stay... and you learn why the pattern fits you like your father did."

Pattern.

Her father's word.

"What do you know about my dad?"

A soft inhale.

Amused.

"Everything that matters."

He smiled when he said it. She could hear it.

Then—

"Consider this a courtesy call."

Silence.

Lights steadied.

Band kept playing.

Crowd blissfully unaware.

Theo reached her first. "Riley? Talk to me."

Mara followed. "Please say something before I start screaming."

Riley swallowed. "He talked to me. On comm. He knows things... about my dad."

Theo's face changed—harder lines, softer eyes. Protective.

This wasn't stage Theo. This was something else.

"Okay," he said. "We're telling Sloan. And Ruiz. And then you're not walking anywhere alone."

Riley didn't argue.

She couldn't.

His words still echoed:

Stay, and you learn why the pattern fits you.

Some part of her—deep behind her ribs—already knew she wasn't going anywhere.

CHAPTER FIVE
The Move

Load-out in Cincinnati dragged like it knew no one wanted it to end.
The show had gone well—clean, loud, euphoric in the way crowds always were when they didn't know how close they'd come to disaster.

Riley had watched the pit from stage left once—an ocean of faces lit by phone screens, wrists banded in VIP laminates, eyes wet with catharsis. They screamed like it was religion. They filmed like it was evidence.

Fans spilled out into the streets buzzing about songs and outfits and moments that would live forever on shaky phone footage.

Someone would already be posting "Jetstream Cincinnati night 1 FULL" with nine minutes of vertical video and a caption that read *I ASCENDED* like they'd discovered oxygen.

Inside the arena, though, the mood had shifted. The adrenaline had curdled.

Everything sounded sharper at night. Road cases didn't just roll—they slammed. Ratchet straps snapped tight with gunshot cracks. The echo of metal on concrete lingered a half-second too long, like the building itself was reluctant to let anyone leave.

It wasn't superstition. It was acoustics. Concrete loved to hold onto sound. Concrete loved to make everything feel like a confession.

Riley moved on autopilot. Hands moving. Clipboard balanced against her hip. Sharpie uncapped, capped, uncapped again. Case numbers checked, rechecked, crossed out, rewritten when her handwriting went crooked. She knew this rhythm. Had lived inside it for years. Normally it soothed her—the predictability, the order imposed on chaos.

Tonight, it didn't land.

Tonight, order looked like a costume somebody could take off and put back on whenever they felt like it.

Every sound made her flinch just a little too late for anyone to notice but her.

Her ribs buzzed—not constant, not screaming—just enough to keep her keyed in, like a phone vibrating somewhere in another room.

Like a notification you didn't want to open because you already knew it would ruin your night.

The charm was logged and bagged, but the memory of it sat warm in her pocket anyway - wrong now that the building had gone dark, the crowd was gone, there was no longer any excuse for adrenaline.

Warm like skin. Warm like *handled*. Warm like somebody had passed it from palm to pocket and enjoyed the transfer.

Mara clocked it immediately, because Mara clocked everything.

"You're doing the thing," she said, falling into step beside Riley as they walked the dock.

"What thing?"

"The thousand-yard stare, but make it 'tour coordinator who's about to internalize a felony.'"

"I'm fine," Riley said automatically.

Mara snorted. "Kentucky, if that were true, you'd be complaining louder."

Fair.

Mara had been loud earlier— performing normal for the crew like it was part of her job description. But now, when the dock was emptier and the night had teeth, her voice stayed closer to Riley's ear.

They passed under the rig one last time. Riley forced herself not to look up.

She could feel the grid anyway. Could feel the weight of it in the way air sat heavier beneath it. Like the building's throat.

Gravity felt personal tonight. Like it had opinions.

Someone laughed too loudly near the truck line.

The kind of laugh that asked the universe to hit them back.

Someone else swore when a case clipped a wall. A forklift chirped a warning as it backed out of the dock, then stopped short.

A local in a venue polo flinched like the chirp sang *her* name.

Riley's ribs buzzed harder.

She paused.

Mara noticed. "Hey."

"I just—" Riley shook her head. "Nothing. False alarm."

False alarms were still alarms. Riley's body didn't do *maybe* anymore.

Mara didn't argue, but she didn't let it go either. She shifted closer, shoulder brushing Riley's like an anchor.

Load-out always stripped a show down to its bones. No lights. No spectacle. Just infrastructure and exhaustion and the quiet knowledge that everyone would do it all again tomorrow in a different city with a different building and the same risks.

The fans didn't see this part. The part where the magic got shoved back into cases, labeled, chained, and shipped like contraband.

Riley hated that she could now see those risks so clearly.

By the time the final truck door slammed shut—1:04 a.m., according to Sloan's watch—the night felt stretched thin.

Time did that on tour. It didn't pass. It smeared.

Sloan stood at the edge of the dock, arms crossed, posture rigid in the way of someone holding herself together by force of will alone.

Sloan's phone kept lighting up in her hand—tiny little bursts of corporate apocalypse. Riley saw the screen once: a calendar reminder, a missed call, an email subject line in all caps. Sloan swiped it away like she could erase reality.

"That's it," Sloan said. "We're clear."

No one cheered.

Crew drifted toward the buses in small clusters, voices low, laughter muted. The easy camaraderie of earlier legs had been replaced with something watchful. Like everyone was waiting for the other shoe to drop and didn't want to be the one standing under it.

A few fans still lingered at the barricade outside the dock gate—hoods up, signs drooping, mascara smudged. They looked exhausted and holy. One of them held a marker like a weapon, ready to autograph-proof their devotion. One of them started crying when a bus door opened and then cried even harder when she realized it was the crew bus.

Mara hooked an arm around Riley's shoulders, steering her toward the bus lot. "Okay," she said lightly. "Honest check-in. Are you okay, or are you 'tour okay'?"

Riley huffed. "What's the difference again?"

"Tour okay means you're actively spiraling, but you can still answer emails."

Riley's phone buzzed in her pocket. Three new notifications. One from a group chat labeled *CREW CHAOS*. One from an unknown number she refused to open. One from a calendar she didn't remember subscribing to.

Riley considered that. "Then yeah. Tour okay."

Mara stopped walking.

That alone was enough to make Riley look at her.

Mara's expression softened, humor giving way to something sharper, more real. "That wasn't an answer."

For a second, Mara looked tired in a way eyeliner couldn't hide.

Before Riley could muster a better one, a presence joined them—solid, quiet, immovable.

Taj.

He moved like a door closing. Like the end of a hallway.

"You're not sleeping on Crew Bus One tonight," he said.

Riley blinked. "What?"

"Orders," Taj said. "Sloan. Ruiz. Management. Anyone who still believes in liability."

The way he said *liability* made it sound like a curse word.

"I don't need special—"

"You're moving to the band bus," Taj cut in, tone final. "Now."

Something cold slid down Riley's spine.

"This is because of... him," she said quietly.

Taj didn't pretend otherwise. "Because of the voice. Because of the cooler. Because someone tried something today and didn't get what they wanted."

63

Because the machine had noticed she was looking back.

Mara, never one to miss an opportunity to cope via sarcasm, clapped her hands once. "Well! Love a promotion. Does the band bus come with better snacks? Because if not, this is emotional damage."

Taj ignored her, eyes on Riley. "You don't sleep alone tonight."

Riley swallowed. "Okay."

The word felt heavier than it should have.

It tasted like surrender. It tasted like strategy. It tasted like *fine, you win this round*.

Mara didn't look surprised. She'd been clocking Taj's posture, the tightened perimeter, the way security had quietly reoriented itself around Riley without announcing it.

"For security's sake," Mara said calmly, already shifting her weight, "she's not moving buses by herself."

Taj's gaze flicked to her. Not irritation. Assessment.

He nodded once.

"Crew clears together," he said. "You grab your things. Both of you."

It wasn't permission.
It was procedure.

Riley exhaled.

She detoured briefly onto Crew Bus One to grab her backpack. The interior felt different now—too quiet, too familiar, like a place she'd already outgrown without realizing it.

Bunks with curtains drawn. Footsteps soft. Someone whispering on a call in the back lounge like the bus was a confession booth. The air smelled like heat and socks and a lemon cleaner fighting for its life.

She tugged her bag from under the bunk, paused, then zipped it harder than necessary.

Her ribs buzzed faintly, urging her back toward the door.

Not fear. Direction.

Outside, the night air was damp and cold. Bus engines idled in a low, constant hum. The band bus loomed larger than she remembered, lights on inside, a pocket of warmth in the dark lot.

It looked less like transportation and more like a moving fortress—until you remembered fortresses could be breached.

The door opened before Taj could knock.

Theo stood there, hoodie pulled on, freshly showered, eyes alert despite the hour.

"You're with us," he said.

Not a question.

The words landed like a hand on her shoulder. Not ownership. Not control. Just *you're not alone*.

Riley hesitated. "Is that—"

"Yeah," he said reassuringly, stepping aside. "Come in."

The band bus felt lived-in. Softer lighting. The faint smell of detergent and coffee and something herbal Drew probably swore cured anxiety.

Something citrus. Something mint. Something that had no business trying to fix anything this big.

Jax was half-asleep on the couch, phone balanced precariously on his chest.

The screen was still open to a fan video. Caption: *HE LOOKED AT ME*. Like it was evidence in a trial.

Rowan tapped out a rhythm at the table, headphones on. Asher poked his head out of the bunk hallway and grinned.

"Oh good," Asher said. "The snack boss has arrived."

"I am a human being," Riley said.

"Debatable," Asher replied cheerfully.

Theo shot him a look. "Be normal."

"I don't know how," Asher said.

Drew wandered out with a mug of tea. "Is this a sleepover? Do we braid hair?"

"No," Mara said, already dropping her pillow onto an empty bunk. "But if anyone snores, I'm starting fights."

She said it like she meant it. She always meant it.

Riley lingered near the doorway, suddenly aware of herself in a way she hadn't been all night.

Theo noticed. "You okay?"

"No," she said honestly. "But I'm here."

He nodded, like that was enough.

Theo didn't try to fix it. He just made space for it. That was its own kind of dangerous.

Taj laid out the rules quietly. Where she'd sleep. When she'd lock the door. What channel to keep her radio on. Riley listened, nodded, absorbed it all without protest.

Sloan's voice crackled once over the comm—tight, controlled: a reminder about wake time, lobby call, next city. Nothing about fear. Everything about momentum.

When the bus finally rolled, lights dimming, engine vibrating under her bunk, Riley lay staring at the ceiling.

Somewhere up front, a driver adjusted mirrors. Somewhere outside, security headlights swept the lot. Somewhere in the dark, a fan refreshed their feed, waiting for Jetstream to like a post so they could screenshot proof of being chosen.

Her ribs buzzed once. Slow. Steady.

Not a warning.

A promise.

Riley's phone lit up facedown on the mattress, the glow leaking around the edges like a guilty secret.

She didn't touch it. She didn't have to.

She already knew the sender.

She closed her eyes, knowing one thing with absolute certainty:

The tour had changed.

And so had she.

And the machine—quiet, patient, hungry—had just made its first real move.

CHAPTER SIX
Float

Detroit came at them without ceremony.

No skyline reveal. No poetic arrival. Just gray light bleeding into the bus windows and the low industrial sprawl announcing itself like a held breath.

The city looked like it had been awake all night and hadn't bothered pretending otherwise.

Riley woke before anyone shook her, ribs humming softly, as if the city had tapped on her shoulder and said, *you're up.*

Not an alarm. Not urgency. Just inevitability.

The band bus slowed, air brakes sighing.

She stayed still for a second, listening.

The engine idled. Someone in the back bunk snored like it was a personal vendetta. Drew's tea kettle rattled faintly in the kitchenette as the bus shifted its weight.

Normal.

Which meant nothing.

"Morning," Theo murmured from the aisle, already up, looking like sleep had negotiated a ceasefire at best. "Detroit."

Riley pushed herself upright. "My body doesn't agree."

"None of ours do," he said. "That's how you know it's working."

He handed her a coffee without asking. Black. Too hot. Correct.

Outside, the arena loomed like it had been poured from concrete and resentment. The dock doors yawned open, swallowing trucks whole.

No branding. No soft lighting. No corporate optimism. Just a building that existed to hold weight and consequences.

No eucalyptus. No hotel polish. Just raw utility and the kind of building that had seen too much and kept going anyway.

As soon as Riley stepped off the bus, her ribs buzzed.

Not sharp.

Directional.

Like a compass needle snapping into place.

Mara clocked it immediately. "Nope," she said. "Absolutely not. We just woke up. Whatever internal ghost you've got needs to respect business hours."

"I didn't invite it," Riley muttered.

Detroit's loading dock was colder than the others had been, but in a different way. Not damp. Not musty. Just stripped bare. Metal on metal. Diesel without apology. The echo of footsteps rang too cleanly, like the space didn't absorb sound so much as throw it back at you.

The acoustics made every sound feel like a warning.

Forklifts moved fast here. Confident. Union riggers already in place, clipped in, eyes sharp.

These weren't tourists. These were lifers.

These were people who did not mess around with gravity.

Which should have made Riley feel better.

It didn't.

They walked the building.
They always did.

Dock to tunnel. Tunnel to bowl. Bowl to stage. Stage to grid access. Emergency exits. Distro rooms.

Power ran like veins behind locked doors—thick cables, color-coded, humming faintly. The heart of the show lived here. If you knew where to cut it, everything stopped.

Places fans never saw and never thought about but trusted with their lives anyway.

Detroit's tunnels were narrower. Slightly higher ceilings. More gaffer tape holding the world together. The air felt tight, like the building was clenching.

"You're quiet," Mara observed.

"I'm listening," Riley said.

"To what?"

Riley tipped her chin up, eyes tracking the steel overhead. "Everything."

The motors. The chains. The way the air shifted under load.

Mara followed her gaze. "That's not ominous at all."

They passed beneath the mid-stage truss. Riley slowed without meaning to.

Her ribs buzzed harder.

She stopped.

Mara stopped with her.

"What," Mara said, already bracing.

Riley looked up.

Nothing was wrong.

Not visibly.

Not on paper.

Not in the reports.

That was the problem.

Chains were trimmed. Safeties glinted. Motors tagged. Everything checked out exactly the way it was supposed to—the kind of clean that passed inspections and buried liability.

Riley stood stage left, arms folded tight across her chest, watching the backline settle into place. The drum riser sat near the upstage edge, fully loaded—kit mounted, hardware tightened, throne locked in place like it belonged there.

It did belong there.

That didn't make it safe.

Six feet of stage.

Another four feet of riser.

Concrete waiting underneath.

She felt the wrongness before she could name it.

Not fear.

Not panic.

Instruction.

The room was half-awake—the pre-soundcheck hum where nothing was loud yet, but everything was alive. Forklifts beeped. Crew voices bounced off steel. Someone laughed too hard at something that wasn't funny.

And the riser—

It was tilted.

Barely. A fraction off true, like a picture frame no one notices until it finally falls.

Her stomach dropped.

"Hey," Riley said, sharper than she meant to. "Who's on the drum riser?"

Two local union hands glanced over. One didn't bother hiding the irritation.

"We're staged," the taller one said. "Waiting on final mark."

"It's off," Riley said. "It shouldn't be sitting like that."

The shorter one scoffed. "It's locked."

Her ribs flared.

Not warning.

Command.

"No," Riley said. "It's not."

A voice cut in from the floor.

"FOH to stage. About to run low-end sweep. Thirty seconds."

The words hit like a gunshot.

Riley's head snapped up. "WAIT—"

Too late.

The subs came online.

Not loud.

Not musical.

Just a low-frequency test tone—the kind you feel in your teeth before you hear it.

The deck didn't shake.

It breathed.

Soundcheck started the way it always did—controlled noise, organized chaos, the building slowly waking up under load.

Drum world went first.

The riser was already locked into its upstage position when Drew climbed up without ceremony. Eight-by-eight steel frame. Casters engaged. Deck plates seated. Hundreds of pounds before a single piece of backline moved.

Then the kit did.

Drew's setup wasn't subtle. Double kick. Rack toms. Floor toms big enough to bruise toes by existing. Cymbals layered high and wide. Hardware dense and unforgiving.

Fully dressed, the kit alone pushed past five hundred pounds.

Add Drew.

Add motion.

Add violence.

The riser took it.

Until it didn't.

The first kick hit.

Then another.

Then both.

The sound wasn't loud yet — just physical. Low and insistent. The kind that traveled through steel before it reached ears.

The riser shifted.

Not enough to see.

Enough to feel.

Riley stopped walking.

When Drew leaned fully into the pattern — legs driving, arms loose, body gone into muscle memory — the vibration changed.

Not stronger.

Directional.

Her ribs lit up.

Vector.

She looked upstage.

The back edge of the riser was bare.

No rail.

Temporary safety should've been clamped there during soundcheck — standard practice until final trim. Someone hadn't put it back.

That alone was bad.

Then the riser kept moving.

Not fast.

Not dramatic.

A slow, continuous drift — measured, almost polite — easing backward inch by inch as vibration gave gravity permission.

Drew didn't notice.

Why would he? His whole body was pitched forward — arms working, legs pistoning, spine committed to the kit. If the platform went, it wouldn't slide out from under him.

It would tip.

Backwards.

Six feet down.

Concrete.

Head first.

With the kit following.

"STOP," Riley shouted.

Her voice cut clean through the room.

Drew froze mid-pattern, sticks hovering.

"What?" Sloan snapped over comms.

"The riser," Riley said, already moving. "KILL LOW END. NOW."

FOH cut the subs.

The vibration dropped.

Momentum didn't.

The riser crept another inch.

That's when Taj saw it.

Not the movement — the continuation.

He moved without hesitation, closing the distance in three strides and throwing his weight into the upstage frame. Boots skidded as he braced, shoulder driving steel back against its own inertia.

Metal screamed — not from impact, but from resistance. From motion being forced to stop.

The back casters hovered just shy of the edge.

Stillness slammed down.

Drew turned slowly, eyes wide as he took in where he was sitting.

"Oh," he said quietly.

Sloan was already there. "Nobody touches anything. Riley."

Riley dropped to her knees.

Hands flat on the deck. She didn't look at the edge.

She looked underneath.

Casters locked.

Pins seated.

Frame true.

That was the lie.

She pressed her fingers against the isolation puck beneath the upstage caster.

It slid.

Not freely.

Just enough.

Her mouth went dry.

The puck was correct — size, placement, rating. Anyone glancing under the frame would've cleared it without a second thought.

But someone had altered it.

A thin, nearly invisible layer — polymer or gel — added between puck and deck. Low-friction. Compressible. Clear.

Static load? Fine.

Push test? Fine.

Sustained vibration with directional force?

It floated.

Riley leaned back on her heels.

"This wasn't going to happen during soundcheck," she said.

Sloan's voice went cold. "Explain."

"When Drew plays full out, his kick pattern drives backward force," Riley said. "The riser wasn't meant to roll. It was meant to drift. To float. Slow enough that nobody clocks it until gravity finishes the job."

Drew swallowed.

"And the rail?" Sloan asked.

Riley looked up.

"Had to be gone," she said. "Otherwise the frame would've stopped short. This was timed."

Ruiz's voice came over comms, low and exact. "He wanted it during the show."

"Yes," Riley said. "When the crowd masked the sound. When motion felt intentional. When Drew wouldn't stop playing."

Taj stayed braced against the riser, jaw tight. "That would've killed him."

Riley nodded once.

"And the kit," she added. "On top of him."

No one spoke.

Finally Sloan exhaled. "Strip it. Full teardown. New casters. New pucks. New rails. Nothing original touches this stage again."

She turned to Riley. "You caught it."

Riley didn't feel triumphant.

She felt measured.

As the crew swarmed, Drew climbed down slowly, hands shaking just enough to notice. He stopped in front of her.

"You saved my life," he said.

Riley looked at the altered puck one last time.

Her ribs buzzed again.

Not fear.

Recognition.

This wasn't the accident.

This was rehearsal.

The day went on.

Soundcheck was tight. The riser held. The show ran clean.

The crowd screamed. Phones rose.

Jetstream detonated the room like it always did.

No one knew how close they'd come to watching a funeral.

But Riley never stopped watching.

And when Detroit finally disappeared behind the bus that night, her ribs buzzed once more — not fear.

Recognition.

This wasn't the moment he'd planned.

Not even close.

This had been a test.

A rehearsal.

A warning.

There were bigger rooms coming. Bigger failures waiting.

Riley lay in her bunk in the dark, shoes kicked off, everything else still on. The bus hummed beneath her — steady, familiar — carrying them toward the next city.

She stared at the ceiling until her eyes burned.

Then, without warning or permission, tears slid sideways into her hairline. Quiet. Unimpressive. The kind you didn't wipe away because no one was watching.

She didn't sob. She didn't break.

She just let it happen.

After a minute, it stopped.

Riley rolled onto her side, pulled the blanket up, and breathed like someone who still had a call time in the morning.

By the time sleep took her, her ribs were quiet again.

Not calm.

Just waiting.

CHAPTER SEVEN
Chicago Doesn't Care

Chicago didn't rise so much as press in.

The skyline appeared between buildings as the tour buses crawled through downtown streets never meant for vehicles that long, that heavy, that full of people who hadn't slept properly in weeks. Glass and steel loomed close on either side, reflections stacking until Riley couldn't tell which buildings were real and which were just the city admiring itself.

Five buses in convoy.

Band. Crew. Gear. Lives packed into rolling black capsules.

The lead bus braked hard.

Not emergency—just Chicago.

Riley's shoulder bumped the wall beside her. She didn't bother swearing. No one did anymore. They were too tired for dramatics.

Mara sat across the aisle with her hoodie pulled low, sunglasses on despite the gray morning. She looked like someone who had gone past exhaustion and wrapped around to defiance.

"Remind me why we agreed to hotels," Mara muttered.

"Because the label hates joy," Asher called from somewhere behind them. "And loves receipts."

Taj's voice came over the bus intercom, calm but clipped. "We're threading a needle here. Stay seated."

The buses eased forward again, mirrors inches from parked cars, pedestrians stopping to stare like they were watching an aquarium glide past.

Riley watched reflections slide along the tinted glass—faces, traffic lights, fragments of people who would never know how close they were to a moving city inside a vehicle.

Her ribs buzzed.

Not sharp.

Not urgent.

Just a steady, unwelcome awareness— like static beneath her skin.

Chicago didn't feel hostile.

It felt uninterested.

And that was worse.

The hotel loading zone wasn't really a zone—just a negotiated truce between city planning and reality. Buses idled half in the street while security argued politely with a man in a vest who clearly hated all of them.

Riley stepped down onto concrete still damp from last night's rain. The air smelled like metal and old water and something electrical that never quite left cities this size.

The lobby doors slid open.

Inside was marble, glass, and the kind of calm money bought when it didn't want to see consequences.

Everything echoed.

The crew flowed in automatically— black clothes, backpacks, Pelican cases rolling like obedient animals. Hotel guests pretended not to stare while absolutely staring.

Someone whispered a name Riley didn't recognize.

She ignored it.

That was part of the job now.

Theo appeared at her shoulder without announcement. "You good?"

"Define good," she said.

He smiled faintly. "You're upright."

"Low bar."

They crossed the lobby together. Taj and another security guard fanned out ahead, not aggressive, just present.

Riley clocked it automatically.

Security presence had increased.

No announcement. No briefing yet.

Just... more bodies where there hadn't been before.

They were halfway to the elevators when Riley felt it.

Not fear.

Not danger.

A misalignment.

The lobby had a rhythm—rolling luggage, murmured conversations, the soft chime of elevators arriving.

And then there was a gap.

A man stood near the far wall, half turned away, looking at nothing in particular.

He wasn't doing anything wrong.

That was the problem.

No phone.

No bag.

No hotel confusion.

Just standing there like he was early for an appointment that hadn't arrived yet.

Riley slowed.

Her ribs buzzed—not louder, but tighter.

Theo noticed instantly. "What?"

She didn't answer. She didn't want to point.

The man shifted his weight. Just enough to catch her reflection in the glass.

Their eyes met.

He didn't flinch.

Didn't look away.

Didn't smile.

He looked... satisfied.

Like he had confirmed something.

Then he turned and walked—not toward the doors, not toward the desk—but through a side corridor marked **STAFF ONLY**.

No one stopped him.

Riley exhaled sharply.

"Riley," Theo said quietly. "Talk to me."

"He doesn't belong here," she said.

Theo followed her gaze to the corridor. "You sure?"

"Yes."

They reached the elevators.

Mara glanced between them. "Why do you both look like someone just rearranged reality?"

Taj appeared beside them. "What did you see?"

Riley hesitated.

Then: "A man. Not crew. Not guest. He knew where he was going."

Taj's jaw tightened almost imperceptibly. "Where?"

"Staff corridor. East wall."

Taj tapped his comm once. "Eyes on east corridor."

The elevator arrived.

They got in.

The doors closed.

No one spoke until they were moving.

Mara finally said, "Cool. Love that. Chicago ghosts."

Riley's ribs didn't stop buzzing.

The room was quiet in the way hotels specialized in—thick curtains, padded silence, neutrality pretending to be safety.

Riley dropped her bag and stood still.

Everything was where it should be.

Too much so.

Theo leaned against the doorframe, watching her—not intrusively, but attentively. "You're still listening."

"I didn't feel him leave," Riley said.

"Who?"

"The man," she replied. Then shook her head. "That sounded insane."

Theo didn't argue. "You don't usually say things like that unless you believe they are true."

She sat on the edge of the bed. The mattress dipped obediently.

Her ribs buzzed again.

Lower.

Steadier.

Like something had settled.

A knock came at the door.

One knock.

Pause.

One knock.

Taj's pattern.

Theo opened it without hesitation.

Taj stood there with another security guard and a hotel supervisor who looked like he wished he'd taken the day off.

"We pulled access logs," Taj said. "Someone badged into staff areas ten minutes before you arrived."

Riley looked up. "Who?"

The supervisor swallowed. "That's the thing. It's not assigned."

Theo straightened. "Meaning?"

"Meaning," the man said carefully, "the badge exists in the system, but it doesn't belong to anyone currently on payroll."

Riley closed her eyes briefly.

Her ribs went quiet.

Not relief.

Confirmation.

"He's already inside the machine," she said.

Taj nodded once. "That's what I was afraid of."

Mara crossed her arms. "So we're not imagining things."

"No," Taj said. "We're just late to the realization."

Theo looked at Riley. "You didn't chase him."

"No," she said.

Good, her body seemed to say.

Very good.

The supervisor cleared his throat. "We'll increase floor security."

Taj didn't look at him. "You'll do more than that."

The man nodded quickly.

When the door shut again, the room felt smaller.

Not trapped.

Contained.

Theo sat on the opposite bed. "You okay?"

Riley stared at the carpet.

"I don't like that he knew I'd notice," she said.

Theo didn't answer right away.

Then: "Then don't give him anything else."

Her ribs buzzed once.

Agreement.

Chicago moved outside the window, uncaring and immense.

The tour had rolled into another city.

And somewhere inside it, something had already learned her name.

CHAPTER EIGHT
Blackout

Chicago's arena woke up angry.

Not loud-angry or chaotic-angry.

Tense angry.

Like the building had read all their emails and found them lacking.

Like it had an opinion about liability.

The second Riley stepped off the SUV into the loading dock, her ribs buzzed.

Not a stab.

Not a warning.

A tap.

Present. Aware.

"Oh, absolutely not," Mara said immediately. "Tell your internal ghost to stand down. I'm tired."

"I can't control it," Riley muttered.

"Have you tried?" Mara snapped, yanking on nitrile gloves like she intended to fistfight destiny.

Mara's coping mechanisms came in two flavors: sarcasm and violence. Sometimes both at once.

The loading dock pressed in from every side—concrete, steel, motion.
Forklifts screamed in reverse.
Road cases slammed over expansion joints like punctuation.
The building didn't care who you were. It just kept moving.

Union riggers moved overhead on the catwalks with grim, competent focus.

This was Chicago.
Nobody here was casual about gravity.

That didn't mean gravity was casual about them.

Sloan stood center floor like a general with a headset, a clipboard, and the violent energy of someone who had already had three arguments and half a panic attack before 9 a.m.

"No one touches a motor without my sign-off," Sloan barked into comms. "I mean it. If you breathe near a hoist without clearance, I will end your day, your week, and your next tour."

Somewhere up in the rafters, a voice yelled, "Ten-four!" with the rattled tone of a man who had just reconsidered his life choices.

Detective Ruiz had a folding table at front-of-house, laptop open, venue maps spread out, a cup of coffee she clearly didn't remember pouring. Her presence shifted the air. This wasn't just a show anymore. It was evidence waiting to happen.

Ruiz didn't *work* shows. She worked disasters. She just happened to be early.

Ruiz glanced up at the grid, then back to Sloan. "For the record," she said, "the person we're tracking doesn't sabotage randomly. He intervenes. Adjusts variables."

"Meaning?" Sloan asked.

"Meaning he doesn't just cause damage," Ruiz said. "He handles outcomes."

Handler.

The word settled into Riley's chest without permission.

Theo crossed the floor with his guitar case slung over his shoulder, hoodie up, curls hiding inside like they didn't trust the building either. As he passed her, his hand brushed her arm.

"You good?" he murmured.

"No," Riley said.

"Cool," he said quietly. "Same."

They were starting to run out of words that meant anything

They walked the building like they had in every city: loading dock to tunnels, tunnels to bowl, bowl to grid access, backstage corridors, emergency exits, catering, production, back to the dock.

Chicago felt wrong.

The lights hummed louder than usual.

The temperature never settled—too cold in one hallway, too warm in the next.

The rig over the stage looked fine on paper, clean on the plot, but her ribs hated it.

"Do not say 'Lexington' out loud," Mara said as they stepped onto the main floor.

"I didn't," Riley said.

"You thought it very loud."

Riley tipped her chin up. The steelwork spiderwebbed high above them—mains, delays, mother grid, downstage truss, points for PA hangs. Motors sat trimmed and tagged. Secondary safeties glinted. Nothing sagged where it shouldn't.

Her ribs buzzed anyway.

Like the building was breathing through her bones.

Mara followed her gaze. "If one more thing falls on this tour, I'm quitting to sell overpriced succulents to influencers."

"You'd hate influencers," Riley said.

"I already do," Mara replied. "I'm prepared."

Sloan joined them under the grid, jaw tight.

"Here's today's fun new rule," she said. "We assume he can touch the system from anywhere. Consoles, dimmers, distro—if it can move, power up, or turn colors, it gets eyes on it."

"You think he'll hit here?" Mara asked.

"He hit Lexington with gravity and Cincinnati with water," Sloan said. "Detroit was hardware. Chicago has more power feeds and more press than all three combined. So, yes, I assume he's salivating."

Riley swallowed. Her ribs thrummed once, like agreement.

Ruiz came up beside them, hands in her jacket pockets.

"Today," Ruiz said, "we prove we can see him, or he proves he can outpace us." Her attention flicked to Riley. "If your ribs sneeze, I want to know."

"That's not an anatomical function," Riley said weakly.

"It is now," Ruiz said.

Ruiz had that rare gift: making insanity sound like policy.

Dressing rooms were the only controllable part of the day.

Riley and Mara bullied the headliner room into submission: overheads off, floor lamps on, humidifier in the corner, plants in the right places—including Tilda, placed dead center on the coffee table like Drew's emotional support altar. Snacks lined up on the sideboard: protein, sugar, pretty lies.

Mara fluffed a pillow with more violence than necessary. "You know what the real horror is? They'll still complain it's too bright."

"Or too dark," Riley said.

"Or the hummus is looking at them wrong," Mara said. "Rockstars."

"How are your ribs?" Riley asked, annoyed at her own question.

"Honestly?" Mara said. "Tense."

"I meant mine," Riley said.

"Oh. Those too."

Her ribs had quieted some. Not fully. It felt like the silence you got when the crowd was in the building but the house lights were still up. Anticipation with nowhere to go.

Theo stuck his head in the doorway, guitar slung over his shoulder like he hadn't fully come down from rehearsals.

"That for us?" he asked, nodding toward the spread.

"No," Mara said. "This is for my food blog. Of course it's for you."

Theo smiled, but it was shallow. Tired.

His eyes landed on Riley.

"Check-in?" he asked.

She considered lying. Her ribs buzzed once as if offended on principle.

"Anxious, slightly haunted, currently upright," she said.

"We'll take it," he answered.

Mara snapped her fingers. "We're not dying in Chicago. I refuse. It's too on-the-nose. If we're getting murdered by a touring pattern, it's going to be at some mid-tier Ohio festival with bad Wi-Fi."

Theo's mouth twitched. "Set the bar high."

Riley's radio crackled. Sloan: "House doors in forty-five. Eyes up."

Riley's ribs replied with a single, clean pulse.

Message received.

The pattern didn't have to shout. It just had to show up.

By the time the house opened, Chicago was a living thing.

Fans flooded in—layers of denim, leather, glitter, eyeliner, signs, anxiety. The concourse hummed. The scent of nacho cheese and spilled beer started warring with the cold concrete.

From the tunnel, Riley watched as floor GA filled, then lower bowl, then upper. Twenty thousand people building a storm.

"Big night," Mara said.

"How can you tell?" Riley asked.

Mara nodded toward the concourse. "There's still a merch line wrapped around the concourse for sizes that are sold out already."

"Tragic," Riley said.

"Biblical," Mara replied.

Somewhere, a label exec was watching the numbers like scripture.

Sloan's voice crackled over comm. "Everyone: this is not the night to be average. If something feels wrong, you say it. I don't care if it's a hunch."

Theo passed them on his way to stage, gently bumping Riley's shoulder with his.

"Don't wander," he said quietly.

"I'm glued to stage left," she replied.

His eyes lingered on her a heartbeat longer than necessary. "Good."

It didn't feel romantic. It felt like a safety harness.

The show launched like a rocket.

Song One hit. The crowd detonated. Light, sound, heat, movement—everyone doing the thing they were built to do.

From her spot at stage left, Riley tracked everything at once: the band's positions, backstage traffic, pyro hits, motor trim, audio meters.

Her ribs buzzed lightly, like background noise.

Like the quiet vibration of an alarm you didn't want to name.

Then Song Two started.

And everything went wrong.

It was nothing at first.

An upstage motor blipped—barely. A quick, unnatural tremor that made one section of truss twitch half an inch.

Riley's ribs punched her.

"Sloan," she snapped into comms. "Upstage left—motor thirty-seven just twitched. It shouldn't be live."

"That motor's parked and double-isolated," Sloan shot back. "If it's moving, the building is lying to me."

Another tremor. This time downstage right—a subtle, too-smooth dip, exactly within tolerances, exactly wrong.

The crowd didn't notice.
The band didn't notice.
But every rigger in the building suddenly had their eyes on the steel.

Mara's voice dropped. "I hate that. I hate that with my whole soul."

Riley's heart hammered. "He's touching the system."

"Chase," Ruiz radioed from FOH, voice low and deadly. "What are you feeling?"

"Like Lexington learned to use a computer," Riley said.

Like gravity hired IT.

The next second, it stopped.

Everything steady.
Everything perfect.
Too perfect.

Her ribs didn't buy it. Neither did she.

She glanced toward FOH. Ruiz was a steady outline in the middle of the tech nest, eyes lifted toward the rig, headset cable coiled at her hip like a leash she refused to drop.

Theo, mid-verse, shifted his weight, turned just enough that Riley could see him looking for her in the wing.

She raised one hand to let him know she was there.

He exhaled. She could see it from thirty feet away.

And then the stage power went out.

Not the whole building.
Not life safety.
Not the emergency aisle beacons.

The stage.
The show rig.

Every wash, beam, profile, blinder, LED tile, and truss light died in unison.

The main PA went mute in a clean, surgical cut.
The band's in-ears cut to hard silence.

Twenty thousand fans gasped as one.
Then the phones came up.
A galaxy.

Thousands of screens rose over heads like bioluminescent plankton.

Theo froze on the thrust, guitar mid-strum. Jax stood center, mic in hand, suddenly nothing but a silhouette rimmed by phone light. Asher started laughing out of sheer panic and then slapped a hand over his own mouth.

On comms, chaos exploded.

"What the hell just—"

"Check mains—"

"Is that a generator trip—"

"House still has juice—"

"Is FOH dead—"

"Who killed the rail—"

"Talk to me, talk to me—"

Someone screamed a curse word so creative it deserved a Grammy.

Riley's ribs didn't buzz now. They roared.

The Handler's voice slid through her headset under the mess.

The calm precision of it—the control—made Ruiz's word snap into place.

"Better, isn't it?" he murmured. "You see more when the show stops pretending."

Her lungs forgot how to function.

"I didn't patch you," she whispered, too quietly for anyone else on channel. "You're not on comm."

"You hear me anyway," he said. "That's what matters."

His voice wasn't loud. It didn't have to be. It lived in the quiet spaces between her thoughts.

Up on the catwalk, two more motors moved.

Slow. Controlled.

A downstage lighting truss dipped just enough to be visible to trained eyes, not enough to risk a fall.

A house rigger yelled from the grid. "Those chains are slaved out. That is not us."

Sloan's voice came over comm, sharp enough to cut steel. "Somebody kill show control and give me hard manual. I want emergency mode only. Now."

Riley's hands shook on her clipboard.

"You could drop it," she whispered. "You could drop everything."

"I don't want to drop it," the Handler replied. "Not yet. You're still in it."

Like a bead on a wire. Like a note on a staff.

The house emergency work lights flipped on, bathing the bowl and the stage in flat, industrial white. The monster under the makeup.

Theo's head turned sharply toward stage left.

He couldn't hear the Handler.
But he could see Riley's face.

And whatever he saw there scared him more than the blackout.

Jax stepped up to his dead mic out of muscle memory, then caught himself. He glanced at Rowan, then Drew, then back at the sea of phones. He threw his arms out in a half-joking shrug.

Chicago screamed.

They thought it was part of the show.

Within seconds, someone in the upper bowl started a chant. "JETSTREAM! JETSTREAM!" It rolled across the arena in waves.

The Handler's voice in Riley's ear smiled without needing a mouth.

"You see?" he said. "They'll turn anything into a story that flatters them. People love thinking they're in on the bit."

"Why?" Riley's throat scraped around the word. "Why this?"

"Because this is the one thing you can't fake," he said. "Power, on and off. That's all a show is."

Crew scrambled around her—stage techs checking cables, electricians on their knees at distro racks, audio scrambling at monitor world. Mara squeezed Riley's jacket sleeve so hard it hurt.

"Stay here," Mara hissed. "Do not move. If you faint, I will drag you into catering and lie about it."

"Can you stop doing bits?" Riley whispered back. "He's talking to me."

Mara went still. "Is it the same voice?"

"Yes."

"Cool," Mara said tightly. "Hate that. Totally hate that."

"Leave the tour," the Handler said, conversational. "You walk away, the power stays on. You stay? I start testing the load limits."

"I'm not your damn QA department," she snapped—out loud, before she could stop herself.

Theo's brow furrowed, catching that.

The crowd roared louder.

They still thought they were watching a show.

Riley knew better.

She was standing inside a crime scene.

And the crime had perfect acoustics.

The arena's sound system came back to life in stages.

First, a low hum at FOH.

Then a few test pops.

Then the mains flickered on at a safe volume.

House lights stayed at partial.

Stage rig remained dark.

Sloan's voice came over comm, calm in the way only rage could be calm.

"Okay. We're in emergency concert mode," she said. "No automated lighting. No moving truss cues. We're running this like it's 1994 and electricity was invented yesterday. No one touches a motor cue. The only thing that moves on that stage now is people."

Jax took the cue, stepping to the edge of the thrust and leaning into the newly returned mic.

"Alright, Chicago," he said. "So. That was not planned. But since you all look insanely good lit by your phones, we're going to pretend it was. You with me?"

The crowd screamed their consent.

"Cool," Jax said. "We're doing the rest of this the old-school way. Less robots, more us."

He turned, nodded once. Drew clicked sticks. Theo's fingers found home on the fretboard. Asher grinned like an idiot.

The music crashed back in.
The show went on.

And Riley stood with her hand on her ribs, feeling the buzz lower, like he'd taken his fingers off the dimmer.

"The pattern likes an audience," Ruiz said quietly in her ear. "He wanted you to see exactly how much he can touch without killing anyone."

"Yet," Riley breathed.

"Yet," Ruiz agreed.

When they finally hit the last chord, confetti cannons misfired their sad little shreds, more out of stubbornness than design.

The crowd left euphoric, buzzing about "that insane blackout thing" as if it were a bonus track, not a warning.

Load-out started slower than usual. The adrenaline crash hit hard.

Riley checked lines, rail paths, deck traffic—but she moved like she was underwater. Everything went through her ribs first.

The Handler had gone quiet.

That was almost worse.

Quiet meant he was satisfied. Quiet meant he was planning.

She was heading up the ramp to stage to collect discarded setlists when something glittered by the drum riser.

At first she thought it was a bit of foil. Confetti. Trash.

Then her ribs buzzed, sharp and focused.

She crouched.

Another charm.

Same delicate silver. Same tiny music note.

Placed at the corner of the riser where she'd stood during changeover that afternoon, arguing with a local about cable runs.

Someone had to climb stairs and weave around cases to drop it exactly there.

Someone who knew where she'd been. Where she'd stand.

Where she'd circle back to when the show ended.

"Don't touch it," Mara said from behind her.

Riley was already holding it.

It was cold.

Not arena-floor cold.

Refrigerator cold.

Like it had been waiting in someone's pocket. Like it had been carried here on purpose.

"Chase," Sloan's voice barked from the wings. "Step away from anything that's glinting, humming, or emotionally charged. Ruiz wants eyes on any of his calling cards before you smudge them with your guilt."

Riley stood, the charm resting in her palm.

"Too late," she said. "He already got my fingerprints."

Ruiz appeared out of nowhere, as usual.

"Let me see," she said.

Riley held out her hand. The charm sat in the center of her palm like punctuation.

"The same?" Ruiz asked.

"Looks like the Lexington one," Mara said. "And the one by the cooler."

"Weight, size, cut," Ruiz murmured. "Custom. Same maker."

"Does that help?" Riley asked, voice sharper than she meant. "Are we going to find him on Etsy?"

Mara made a strangled sound that might've been a laugh if fear wasn't actively strangling it.

"It helps prove continuity," Ruiz said. "He wants us to know these belong together."

"Like a set," Riley said.

"Like a pattern," Ruiz corrected.

She dropped the charm into an evidence bag and sealed it.

"Production office," Sloan said. "Now. All of you."

And above them, somewhere in the steel, the building kept humming—like it was enjoying the show.

CHAPTER NINE
Motel Hell

The night they left Chicago, the sky decided to be dramatic.
Not romantic dramatic. Not poetic. More like weather channel anchor at 2 a.m. clutching a radar map dramatic.

Lightning stitched the horizon in quiet, far-off pulses—like the Midwest was taking selfies.

Riley watched the city lights slide away in the band bus window, a smear of gold and red against dark glass. The highway swallowed them. The convoy fell into formation: crew buses, band bus, truck packs hauling truss and video wall through the midwestern dark.

The kind of moving fortress that still somehow felt exposed. Like a parade nobody asked for.

Inside the bus, everything was soft-lit and deceptively calm — the kind of calm that only exists when you're so exhausted your body forgets how to panic correctly. The lounge carried that familiar tour mix: stale coffee in a paper cup, clean laundry warmed by the heaters, and the faint, expensive sharpness of Theo's soap — like someone had tried to scrub "normal" back onto a night that wouldn't take it.

Her ribs had been buzzing on and off since the blackout.
Not constant. Not sharp.
Just enough to remind her the voice from Chicago had reached the grid and liked what he found.

Like a cat that learned your house has birds.

Mara snored softly in the bunk across from her, one hand dangling out like she'd fallen asleep arguing with gravity. From the front lounge, she could hear the low murmur of Jax and Asher debating whether a particular crowd chant had been flattering or vaguely threatening. Rowan's muffled laugh cut through every so often — the kind of laugh that sounded like he was trying not to wake the dead. Theo's guitar traced faint chords under the bus noise—a quiet loop of

sound that never quite settled into a song.
Not because he couldn't finish it.
Because finishing things felt like tempting
fate.

Because endings were where the
pattern liked to hide.

Riley lay on her back in the narrow
bunk and watched the small strip of ceiling
just above her face. The bus ceiling had tiny
scuffs and screw heads and the occasional
faint stain from a life lived too fast. She'd
stared at that ceiling for hours of her life
already and somehow it still felt like a new
place every night.

Tonight should have been simple: leave
Chicago, drive through the night, roll into
Nashville mid-morning, park at Bridgestone
for two days off before two sold out days of
chaos.
Simple.

Nashville: where everybody smiled
while holding knives and NDAs.

Except her ribcage felt like someone
had taken up tapping as a hobby in there.

She checked her phone.
No new messages from Ruiz.

No new unknown numbers.
That almost made her more nervous.

Silence wasn't peace. Silence was loading.

A buffering wheel you didn't want to see.

She shoved her headphones in, trying to drown the buzzing under music. It didn't work. The rhythm of the bus, the steady growl of the engine, the occasional thump from a truck hitting a pothole—they all merged into a low-grade tension that curled in the base of her skull like a fist.

She tried doomscrolling instead. Her brain rejected it the way a body rejects spoiled food.

Around 2:30 a.m., the bus lurched. Not the usual lane shift. A harder jolt. Something big.
Something sudden.
The kind of motion that makes your stomach float for half a second before it drops back into your body like it's disappointed in you.

Mara's curtain ripped open. "If we died, I'm going to be so annoyed."

"We didn't die," Riley said, pushing herself upright.

Mara squinted at her, hair in every direction, mascara slightly smudged like she'd tried to sleep and failed out of spite. "How do you know?" she grumbled. "This could be hell."

"If this is hell, the mattresses would be much worse," Riley said.

"Give it time," Mara muttered, like hell took notes.

A shout drifted from the driver's seat, muted through the door. Then Taj's voice: "Everybody hold on."

The bus slowed.
The engine downshifted. The familiar hum turned into a low grumble as they eased off the highway. The change in motion was immediate — from smooth vibration to jittery rattle — like the bus itself had stepped from asphalt onto regret.

"Why are we stopping?" Asher called from the lounge. "I didn't emotionally prepare for roadside murder tonight."

The bus pulled onto rougher pavement—an exit ramp, Riley guessed. The motion changed again: concrete seams, a shallow pothole, the subtle sway of a vehicle that absolutely did not want to be here.

Mara swung her legs out of the bunk. "Well," she said. "This feels ominous."

"Everything feels ominous to you," Riley replied.

"Yeah," Mara said. "And look how often I'm wrong."

The bus finally rolled to a heavier stop. Engine still running, but idle.
That idle sounded different in the middle of the night. It wasn't just a machine waiting. It was a heartbeat refusing to slow down.

Taj's voice came loud enough for everyone to hear. "Everyone decent? We've got a situation."

That sentence was never followed by anything good.

They gathered in the front lounge, bleary-eyed and mismatched.

Tour people never looked more human than they did in the middle of the night — stripped of stage blacks, laminated confidence, and "we're fine" performance.

The lounge lights were dim, and everyone's faces looked softer under them, like sleep had tried to claim them and gotten interrupted by the universe.

The band looked like a group of guys who had accidentally wandered into an HR meeting.

Theo appeared in sweatpants and a T-shirt, curls smashed on one side from sleep and a red line across his cheek from the pillow. Jax wrapped himself in a hoodie like it was a blanket with branding. Rowan leaned on the counter, eyes narrowed. Drew clutched a mug he absolutely did not have time to brew. Asher, infuriatingly, looked like he'd just finished a light workout with a glam squad.

Asher's gift was being alarming in any lighting.

Taj stood near the door, jaw tight.

"Short version," he said. "There's a wreck on the interstate about ten miles ahead of us. Multi-vehicle. Hazmat cleanup. They're diverting traffic, but the backup goes for miles. We either sit on the shoulder of a highway until mid-morning or we find somewhere else to stop."

The word hazmat landed like a metal object dropped into a quiet room.
Not because it was scary in itself.
Because on this tour, everything had started to sound like a setup.

Because "hazmat" could mean chemicals. It could mean fuel. It could mean "somebody made a mess on purpose."

"Somewhere else like where?" Jax asked. "A magical all-night spa with soundproof rooms and complimentary therapy?"

"Welcome to Indiana," Mara said. "We'll be lucky if it's a Shell station with working toilets."

Theo glanced toward the window. Riley followed his gaze. The view outside was a whole lot of nothing: a dark smear of trees, a faint flicker of an exit sign. No city glow. No truck stop neon.
Just black.
Just space.
Just... room for someone to hide.

"Is it safe to sit on the shoulder?" Riley asked.

"Not with trucks crawling through one lane and rubberneckers doing sixty," Taj said. "And not when we're already on somebody's radar."

Nobody had to ask which somebody.

The quiet after that was thick. Everyone knew the truth: they'd stopped being "a band on tour" somewhere around Cincinnati. Now they were a moving target dragging a spotlight behind them.

And the spotlight wasn't stage lighting. It was attention. The kind that didn't clap.

"So, what's the plan?" Rowan asked.

Taj exhaled through his nose. "There's a small town just off this exit. Two miles in. One motel, one diner, one gas station. Drivers are voting for sleep and indoor plumbing. I'm voting for not being visible on a backed-up interstate for six hours."

Mara made a face. "We're staying in a small-town off-ramp motel? Oh good. I was worried we hadn't hit all the horror tropes yet."

Riley's ribs buzzed once, sharp and quick.

Like a cursor blinking. Like: yes. Here.

Theo noticed the way she stiffened. "Kentucky?"

She forced herself to breathe. "It's fine. Just... dramatic bones."

Taj's gaze flicked between them, not missing a thing. "We'll do it controlled," he said. "One property. Buses parked in a cluster. Taj rules apply."

"Taj rules?" Asher asked. "I didn't agree to Taj rules."

"Yes, you did," Taj said. "Every time you signed an insurance renewal.

Sloan's voice cut into the lounge over comms, sharp and already irritated.

"Are we losing time?" she demanded.

Even filtered through a speaker, she sounded like a woman whose schedule had just been personally insulted.

"Not much," Taj said. "We'll catch it tomorrow. Right now the safest move is to get off the highway."

Over comms, Sloan's voice went tight. Riley could picture her glaring out the window like she could intimidate the wreck out of existence. "Fine. Motel. Four hours down, then back on the road. Nobody goes anywhere alone. Nobody announces where we are online. I swear to God, if someone geotags the ice machine—"

"That was one time," Asher said. "And it was a nice ice machine."

"Shut up," Sloan replied.

The decision was made.

Indiana, it was.

Riley's ribs hadn't stopped humming.

The motel appeared out of the dark like a punchline.

Two stories of fading stucco and chipped brick wrapped around a parking lot that had clearly given up. The sign out front flickered "STARLITE LODGE" in half-dead neon, the R and one of the T's gone, so it read "STA LIE LOD E."

"That feels honest," Mara said. "I appreciate the transparency."

The awning over the front office sagged in the middle, as if weighed down by regret. A soda machine near the entrance buzzed like it was possessed. Orange light spilled from the tiny lobby windows.

Orange light was never comforting. Orange light was what horror movies used right before someone made a bad decision.

Riley pressed her palm lightly to her sternum as she stepped off the bus.

Her ribs were louder now.

Not a scream.

Not Lexington.

But a definite, insistent hum.

This place wasn't just sad. It was wrong.

Wrong like the air had been reheated too many times.

She squinted at the parking lot. A few cars that looked permanently installed. A rusting pickup near the far corner. A semi cab without its trailer. Lights glowed in a handful of rooms on the second floor. A man in a stained tank top smoked outside one door, watching the convoy with flat curiosity.

Not excited.

Not scared.

Just... watching. Like he'd seen worse and didn't want to make small talk about it.

"I hate it here," Mara announced.

"You haven't even gone inside yet," Asher said.

"I've seen enough," Mara replied.

Taj gathered them under the awning.

"Rules," he said. "Band, Mara, Riley, and I are on the first floor. Sloan, some department heads, and drivers on the second. Nobody leaves the property. Nobody opens their door unless they know the voice on the other side. Group trips to the lobby or vending machines. You text me if anything feels off."

"Define off," Jax said.

Riley nearly said, My ribs will let you know, but decided that was not a reassuring sentence.

Theo glanced at her instead. "She'll know," he said.

Taj nodded once, like that was already in his playbook.

Sloan marched into the lobby like she owned it.

The lobby smelled like moth balls and maybe something fried.

Not "somebody made bacon earlier." More like "this building has absorbed the idea of grease and never let it go."

A faded print of a lighthouse hung crooked behind the counter. The front desk itself was a laminate rectangle with a bell, a tired credit card terminal, and a jar of keys—actual metal keys on plastic tags, the room numbers written in Sharpie.

Riley eyed the jar. "Oh absolutely not," she murmured. "If a door uses metal keys, there's definitely a dead body in the mattress."

Mara snorted. "There's at least one dead body in this lobby. We just haven't found it yet."

The clerk appeared from a back room: a woman in her seventies with graying hair scraped into a ponytail and a name tag that said MAUDE in peeling letters.

Her expression barely shifted at the sight of forty-something touring personnel, two buses' worth of road cases, and five men who regularly trended on social media.

"Group rate?" Maude asked.

Sloan stepped forward with her most weaponized smile. "Block of twelve rooms," she said. "First floor if possible. We're paying. No parties. No noise complaints. No one will smoke in the rooms. No one will sue you. It's the best night of your life."

Maude blinked at her. "Card?"

Sloan slid a corporate AmEx across the counter like a bribe to the gods.

While Maude processed payment at glacial speed, Riley scanned the lobby.

Flyers for local churches. A rack of maps. A bulletin board with index cards advertising lawn services, car repairs, and "ROOM FOR RENT BY WEEK." A dusty fake ficus in the corner. A small, old-fashioned wall clock ticking just a little too loud.

Her ribs hummed gently in time with it.

Tick. Tick. Tick. Like a metronome that hated her.

Theo sidled closer. "Scale of one to 'we're dying in here,' where you at?" he murmured.

"Somewhere around 'don't take your shoes off,'" Riley said.

131

"Reasonable," he replied.

Maude finally slid a stack of keys across the counter. Actual keys. On red-and-white plastic tags. No keycards, no logs, just the assumption that whoever held the metal owned the room.

"Okay," Sloan said, distributing them like fate. "Band and immediate chaos magnets..." She handed one to Jax. "Room twelve." To Theo, Rowan, Drew, and Asher: "Thirteen, fourteen, fifteen, sixteen. All ground floor, all in a row. Taj..." She passed him a key. "Room eleven, outside corner."

She slapped another key into Mara's hand. "You and Riley. Ten. Right next to Taj. Nobody goes anywhere without telling him first."

Mara looked at the key skeptically. "Feels like a prop from a slasher movie."

"Then don't split up and investigate," Sloan said. "Problem solved."

The hallway to their rooms was a strip of beige carpet and buzzing fluorescents. The walls carried the faint perfume of old cigarettes and industrial cleaner. A vending alcove near the ice machine hummed like it was nursing a grudge.

Their assigned room looked like a woman named Lorraine had decorated it in 1974 and then died in it.

Two beds with floral comforters.
A bolted-down nightstand.
A lamp with a shade that leaned like it had seen atrocities.
Heavy curtains in a brown-and-gold pattern that actively angered Riley's eyes.
A TV the size and weight of a small car perched on a dresser that might once have been wood.

"Oh good," Mara said. "A room with tuberculosis."

Riley dropped her bag on the closest bed and immediately regretted it. "If I turn on a blacklight in here, do I die?"

"Instantly," Mara said. "You'd vaporize. Just a puff of ash and trauma."

The carpet squished faintly under Riley's shoes.
She refused to explore that further.

She walked to the window and yanked the curtains open a few inches. The glass was streaked and slightly fogged between the panes. Through it, she could see the parking lot—a skewed view of the buses, the motel sign flickering, the rusted pickup in the corner.

She could also see the reflection of the room behind her.

Her ribs buzzed.

She studied the window.

Nothing obvious moved.

No shape outside the glass. No shadow across the lot.

"Mara?" she asked.

"Problem?"

"I don't know yet," Riley said.

"Put that on a shirt," Mara replied. "Tour motto."

They did the usual hotel drop-off routine compressed into something more feral.

Mara checked the bathroom. "Shower's questionable. Towels are legal-sized. Sink leaks. Someone carved their initials into the mirror frame in, like, 1983," she reported. "But there's toilet paper, so we stay."

Riley peeled back the comforter. The sheet underneath had that glossy, over-bleached texture of fabric that had lived too long.

"If I find so much as one hair on this pillow, I'm setting the bed on fire," she said.

"Don't," Mara said. "We don't have pyro insurance for this place."

Taj knocked once and opened the door without waiting for an answer. He scanned the room in one movement: door, window, bathroom, two beds, corners, under the dresser.

"You're not staying alone," he said, like it was already decided.

"Obviously," Mara said. "We're co-dependent and deeply emotionally stunted. We know this."

He nodded, satisfied. "Good. Stay put for a bit. We're going to sweep the property. I want eyes on every exit, the back lot, the side alley, and whatever sad patch of grass counts as a courtyard."

"Copy that," Riley said.

Taj's gaze rested on her for a second longer. "You feel anything?" he asked.

Her ribs hummed. "It doesn't feel good," she said. "But it doesn't feel... targeted. Yet."

"That's the best review anything's gotten tonight," he said.

He closed the door behind him with a soft click.

Mara flopped backward onto the bed farthest from the window, arms spread. "This room has seen things," she said. Riley didn't argue.

For a while, nothing happened. Which somehow made everything worse. Because quiet in a motel like this didn't feel like safety. It felt like the building holding its breath. Like the air was waiting for a cue.

Like something backstage right before the curtain went up—except the curtain was a door and the stage was a parking lot in Indiana.

Riley sat on the edge of the bed, shoes still on, scrolling through a text thread with Ruiz.

Made it off highway. Tiny motel. Weird vibes. Nothing specific yet.

Ruiz replied almost immediately.

SEND ME NAME + TOWN.

Riley checked the notepad on the nightstand. The hotel logo at the top read "Starlite Lodge – Exit 23 – Plainfield, IN."

She typed it out.

Three gray dots blinked, disappeared, blinked again.

GOOD. LESS TRAFFIC. HARDER TO LEAVE UNNOTICED, Ruiz wrote. TELL TAJ I SAID HI.

Riley snorted.

She tells you hi, she typed to Taj in a separate thread.

He replied with a thumbs-up emoji, which looked deeply wrong coming from him.

Like seeing your accountant do a TikTok dance.

There was a knock on the door. Three short taps.

Mara rolled onto her side. "Password?"

Theo's voice came through the wood. "Mara is emotionally unavailable and Riley doesn't know how to nap."

"Accurate," Mara said, hopping up. She checked the peephole, then opened the door.

Theo stood in the hallway with Drew and Rowan at his back, each of them holding plastic takeout bags that smelled like fries and something fried that might once have been chicken.

"We raided the diner," Theo said. "Offerings."

"You idiots walked to the diner?" Mara demanded. "Do you have a death wish?"

"It shares a parking lot with the gas station," Rowan said. "We could still see the buses."

"Congratulations," Mara said. "You survived the first level of Indiana."

Drew held up one of the bags. "They gave us extra biscuits. I think they felt sorry for us."

"They should," Mara said. "We're staying here."

Theo's eyes skimmed the room automatically. His gaze lingered a second longer on the window, the bathroom door, the gap under the beds.

"You good?" he asked Riley.

"Define good," she said.

He smirked faintly. "Tour-good. You haven't cried on a stranger yet."

"Then yeah," she said. "I'm fine."

They ate on the beds because there was nowhere else to sit. Fries out of cardboard cartons, biscuits drizzled in something that might legally be called gravy, soda from sweating Styrofoam cups.

Asher appeared a few minutes later, having followed the scent of food like a bloodhound.

"Wow," he said, stepping in. "Love what you've done with the... death trap."

"This decor is a hate crime," Mara said. "The lady at the front desk did this to us personally."

Riley glanced at the walls. "This place has definitely outlived her sense of mercy."

They should have been laughing harder. The jokes landed, but thinner.

Everyone's eyes kept drifting toward the window, the door, the cheap brass lock.

Like the lock was a suggestion, not a boundary.

Riley's ribs buzzed again when the breeze outside shifted and a distant truck rumbled past on the road.

She swallowed hard.

Theo caught it.

"You felt something?" he asked under his breath.

"I feel everything," she whispered back. "That's the problem."

It happened in a sliver of time.

Fifteen minutes maybe. Twenty at most.

After food, after banter. When everyone finally started to sag.

"We should let them sleep," Drew said, gathering trash. "They actually work."

Riley threw a fry at him.

He caught it in his mouth, proud of himself.

One by one, they trickled back out into the hallway. Asher to bother Jax. Rowan to call his sister. Drew to tuck Tilda somewhere she wouldn't be traumatized.

Theo was last to leave.

He lingered at the door, hand on the frame.

"If anything feels off," he said quietly, "call me before Taj."

"Why?" she asked.

"Because Taj will bring a sledgehammer and a police report," Theo said. "I'll bring plausible deniability."

She snorted. "I'll keep that in mind."

He started to step out.

Stopped.

"Hey," he added. "We're not alone out here. Okay?"

"Yeah," she said. "That's kind of the problem."

He left.

Mara turned the deadbolt, slid the chain across, then leaned against the door and exhaled. "I hate this building."

"Same," Riley said.

"You should pee before the shower," Mara replied. "If something goes wrong, I don't want logistics slowing us down."

"Romantic," Riley said.

She grabbed her toiletry bag and went into the bathroom first.

141

The light flickered when she flipped the switch.

She froze.

The buzzing in her ribs jumped.

Riley turned the shower on and didn't step in right away.

She just stood there for a second, letting the hot water pound against tile like it could rinse the day out of her bones. The motel bathroom was small, ugly, functional — the kind of place built for people passing through, not staying long enough to matter.

"Riley," Mara called from the other room. "You good?"

"Yeah," Riley lied. "Just... negotiating with the plumbing."

"Don't look too closely at anything," Mara said. "That's my advice."

She stepped under the spray and closed her eyes.

The water was too hot at first. She didn't move away from it.

She let it run over her shoulders, down her back, over her ribs — over everything that had been tight and buzzing and alert for days. For a minute, she let herself pretend the noise in her body was just exhaustion. Just adrenaline. Just another tour ache that would burn out if she ignored it long enough.

Steam gathered fast.

By the time she shut the water off, the mirror was completely fogged, the room softened into white blur. No edges. No angles. No places to watch.

She wrapped a towel around herself and stepped toward the sink.

Without thinking, she wiped a clear circle in the glass with the heel of her hand.

Her reflection stared back at her — flushed, damp hair pulled back badly, eyes a little too sharp for someone who'd just showered. She didn't recognize herself right away. Not fully.

She leaned closer.

And that's when she saw it.

Not in the cleared circle.

Just outside it.

A shape where the steam hadn't settled.

A thin, precise outline in the fog — clean lines where condensation refused to cling.

Riley's breath caught.

She wiped the mirror wider.

The shape sharpened.

The broken note.

Simple. Deliberate. Exact.

Her ribs buzzed hard.

She lifted her hand and touched the glass.

Her fingers slid — just slightly.

Not water.

Not soap.

Something slick. Clear. Almost invisible.

Vaseline. Or something like it.

Her stomach dropped.

He hadn't scratched it.
He hadn't etched it.

He had drawn it — carefully — with something meant not to show until the room filled with steam.

Riley stepped back like the mirror might reach for her.

"He was in here," she said quietly.

Mara appeared in the doorway instantly. "What?"

Riley pointed.

Mara crossed the room, squinting. Then she swore — low and furious.

"Oh. No. Absolutely not."

"He did it before we got here," Riley said. "Before we ever walked in."

Mara stared at the mirror. "So he knew which room."

"Yes."

"And he knew you'd come in here."

"Yes."

The bathroom felt smaller now. Not invaded — prepared.

A knock sounded at the door.

Two sharp raps.

A pause.

"Taj," his voice came through. "Hallway check. Open up."

Mara unlocked the door immediately.

Taj stepped in, eyes scanning automatically—bathroom, mirror, corners, floor. He stopped when he saw the glass.

"How long has that been there?" he asked.

"Long enough to wait for steam," Riley said.

Taj exhaled once, slow and controlled.

145

"Okay," he said. "Nobody touches anything else."

He tapped his radio. "Sloan. We've got confirmation. He accessed the room before check-in."

A beat.

Then Sloan's voice, sharp and awake. "Explain."

"He drew a symbol on the bathroom mirror with a clear substance," Taj said. "Timed for heat. No forced entry."

Silence on the line.

Then: "I'm looping Ruiz," Sloan said. "But she's not nearby. Lock this floor down. No one moves alone."

Riley's phone buzzed on the counter.

Once.

UNKNOWN NUMBER.

Then stopped.

A voicemail icon appeared.

Mara didn't hesitate. She hit speaker.

Static—clean and deliberate.

Then the voice.

"Nice motel," the Handler said calmly. "Cozy."

Riley's knees weakened. She caught the sink.

"Rooms aren't random," he continued.

The message ended.

The room went silent.

Her ribs screamed.

Taj was already moving, radio up again. "Sloan. He called while we were here."

"Pack," Sloan said immediately. "Nobody sleeps. Ten minutes."

Theo appeared in the doorway, hand still on the frame, eyes already on Riley's face.

"He was in here," Riley said. "He knew exactly when I'd see it."

Theo's jaw set. "We're not staying."

"No," Taj agreed. "We're not."

Sloan's voice cut back in. "Buses roll as soon as people are upright. No exceptions."

They moved fast after that—bags thrown together, boots back on, doors checked twice. The mirror stayed behind, faint smear catching light like an accusation no one could erase.

As Riley stepped into the hallway, she looked once more at the bathroom.

At the place he'd chosen.
Not to scare her.
To prove he could plan.
Her ribs buzzed—not fear.
Calibration.

The hallway felt narrower on the way out.

The air tasted like old smoke and something else now—something metallic at the back of her tongue.

Outside, the parking lot glowed under the harsh wash of sodium lights. The buses looked huge and comforting. Home on wheels.

Riley glanced back over her shoulder as she climbed the steps.

The motel loomed behind them. A rectangle of bad choices and worse carpet. A few long-term residents watched from doorways, smoke curling around their faces. The rusted pickup in the corner lot glinted once as a distant car passed, throwing headlights across its windshield.

For a heartbeat, in that warped reflection of glass and metal, Riley thought she saw him.

Hat.

Height.

Stillness.

Blink, and it was just a battered truck window again.

Her ribs buzzed.

Theo was right behind her on the bus steps, close enough that their shoulders brushed.

"See something?" he asked.

"Yes," she said. "No. I don't know."

He nodded anyway, like that made as much sense as anything else lately.

Taj stood at the bottom of the steps, watching the whole property with the intensity of someone daring the night to move.

"Hey," he called up to Riley. "One good thing."

She almost laughed. "There's a good thing?"

"You never took your shoes off," he said. "That's survival instinct."

She huffed out something almost like a laugh.

The bus door hissed shut.

Engines rumbled to life.

The Starlite Lodge shrank in the side window as they pulled away, neon sign flickering its broken promise: STA LIE LOD E.

As the buses rolled back toward the highway, Riley leaned into the steady vibration of the couch, eyes unfocused on the dark smear of trees sliding past the glass.

Her ribs buzzed once, hard and unmistakable.

The Handler hadn't need to follow them into the room.

He'd chosen it.

Chosen the number. Chosen the mirror. Chosen the exact place she'd stand without thinking.

A message that didn't require witnesses.

Rooms weren't random.

Neither was she.

Mara slid into the seat across from her, reaching out to steal the blanket from Riley's knees.

"You realize," Mara said, voice too casual, "that Nashville is going to be hell."

"I know," Riley said.

Theo dropped into the seat beside her, thigh brushing hers, eyes on the dark blur of the trees.

"Then good," he said. "We'll be ready."

Riley wasn't sure that was true.

But as the convoy merged back onto the interstate, engines humming, taillights ahead and behind them like a guarded line, she knew one thing for certain:

Indiana was rehearsal.
Nashville would be the main act.

And somebody had already bought front row.

CHAPTER TEN
Open Systems

They hit Nashville just after noon—the kind of bright southern sun that pretends nothing bad ever happens there, which was hilarious considering Nashville was built on broken dreams, stolen publishing deals, and bachelorette parties wielding inflatable anatomy like medieval weapons.

The sun hit everything like a spotlight: flattering, unforgiving, and not interested in consent.

The city looked freshly polished for tourists... blue sky, clean lines, glass towers reflecting themselves like they were trying to convince everyone they weren't built on debt. It was a lie the way stage lighting was a lie. A flattering wash. A soft focus. Nashville had learned to glow while it ate people.

It didn't chew, either. It swallowed.

Two blacked out SUVs and a couple 15-passenger vans Sloan had ordered pulled up to the curb outside Bridgestone Arena where the buses would sleep without them. Management insisted the crew and band stay downtown "for convenience." Sloan insisted they stay together "for survival." Taj insisted on shotgun "because I need to see death coming."

Nobody argued with Taj about death anymore. Not after Indiana.

The second Riley stepped out of the SUV, Nashville hit her with spring the way it hit everything—loud, confident, and slightly dishonest.

Not heat. Not summer swamp.

Just that damp April warmth that lived in the seams: the air still cool in the shade, already sticky where the sun touched concrete. Like the city couldn't decide if it wanted to bloom or bruise.

The wind carried honky-tonk ghosts and a faint whiff of fryer oil from somewhere that refused to sleep.

Riley's hair didn't frizz.

It just... gave up an inch of obedience.

Mara squinted at the sky. "This weather is flirting with violence."

Riley adjusted her backpack. "It's Tennessee. It says bless your heart and means good luck surviving."

Theo stepped out behind them, shoulders tight, scanning without looking like he was scanning.

He blinked at the gray-blue sky like it had personally inconvenienced him.

"Is it always like this here?" he asked.

"Like what?" Mara said.

"Like the air is deciding whether to be spring or a warning."

Riley's ribs buzzed once, low and private.

Prediction didn't care about temperature.

Asher pointed at a passing pedal tavern full of screaming women in matching cowboy hats. "Yes."

Rowan nodded grimly. "They migrate here to mate."

Drew squinted at a group of aspiring country singers handing out business cards to uninterested tourists. "This whole block is like a talent show nobody asked for."

Taj surveyed the street with the suspicion of a man who had seen too much. "Eyes up. Broadway is basically Thunderdome with alcohol permits."

And fewer rules.

The street in front of them was a living organism A steady churn of tourists drunk on novelty and immunity, moving in packs like prey that believed volume made them dangerous.

Somewhere, a bachelorette shouted "WOOO" like it was a personality trait. Somewhere else, a busker was murdering "Friends in Low Places" in a key that wasn't listed in any known musical system.

The sound bounced off glass and neon and came back twice as mean.

Riley took a breath she regretted instantly. The air tasted like spilled beer, barbecue, and dreams that needed to go to rehab.

Sloan strode ahead of them, already muttering about PR meetings, label ambushes, and how she had no patience for anyone whose business card said "creative strategist."

The kind of person who said "synergy" and meant "your soul."

The hotel rose up the block—a sleek glass tower entirely too nice for the chaos it overlooked. A building designed to look like money and make compliance feel inevitable. Riley had barely stepped into the lobby before she clocked the swarm.

Managers. Label reps. PR assistants in outfits so curated they practically had sponsorships. Industry dudes with Bluetooth headsets permanently fused to their skulls. Everyone pretending they weren't staring at the band. Everyone pretending they hadn't been waiting in the lobby for forty-two minutes just in case Jetstream walked through.

The whole lobby had the energy of a meet-cute, except nobody here loved anyone. They loved access.

And it wasn't just the staring. It was the micro-math happening behind their eyes. Who can I use?

Who can I introduce myself to?

Who can I pretend I "love the work" of long enough to get a phone number?

Who can I ignore because they look like labor and not leverage?

Riley felt herself categorized in real time. Crew. Invisible. Not worth the pitch. Which, lately, felt like a blessing and a warning.

For five guys from Atlanta, this was the closest thing they had to a hometown industry welcome. Atlanta had become the mecca for movies but Nashville, "Music City", once just known for country music now housed a huge portion of the music industry as a whole. Home base for their management, booking, and PR.

Home base for a thousand smiling predators in clean shoes.

"Smile," Mara muttered. "The sharks can smell fear and low streaming numbers."

"Don't say that," Drew said. "Our last single is doing fine."

"Fine is what labels say when they're deciding whether to ruin your life," she replied.

A label exec in a too-tight blazer intercepted Sloan with a grin that showed too many teeth. "Sloan! Great to see you. We didn't expect the whole team yet."

Sloan did not slow down. "We're here. Please lower your expectations immediately."

The exec laughed like someone had told him to. "We should all get drinks later."

Sloan's smile was knife-sharp. "If by drinks you mean me, by myself, in my room checking emails, sure."

He wilted.

Riley watched the exchange like a stage manager watching a near-miss: impressed, terrified, and taking notes.

Mara whispered to Riley, "She's my hero."

Riley whispered back, "She's everyone's fear."

The lobby smelled like hotel citrus-scented ambition. Everything was clean in the way a showroom was clean—no fingerprints, no humanity. Riley could feel the air conditioning hitting her like a warning she couldn't ignore. The floors were marble. The light was expensive. The vibe said: We host people with money and pretend it isn't blood money.

The kind of lobby where a scream would sound rude.

Theo lingered close—not obviously, but close enough that Taj gave him a look like I'm watching you, Romeo. Theo ignored him and checked that Riley was still beside him.

"You good?" he asked quietly.

The words meant more now.

After Lexington.

After Cincinnati.

After the motel.

Riley nodded even though she wasn't sure. "I'm... aware."

Theo almost smiled. "Tour word for not okay."

"Yeah."

Their rooms were on one secure floor— band, Taj, Sloan, Mara, Riley. No one alone. No exceptions. Everyone could hear someone's voice through a wall if necessary—which, given the last week, meant survival odds increased by at least thirty percent.

Nashville money couldn't buy safety, but it could buy proximity.

Even the elevator ride up felt like theater. A polished mirror world where everyone pretended they weren't trapped in a glass box full of strangers who might sell your worst moment for a sentence in a pitch email. Riley watched a PR assistant's reflection touch up her lipstick like she was repairing the lie in real time.

Riley wondered how many lies the woman had repaired today. How many she'd rehearsed.

Mara and Riley shared a room.

When they stepped inside, Riley nearly cried.

Beds that didn't smell like ghosts. A bathroom not possessed by mildew demons. A window that looked out over downtown instead of a murder cornfield.

And it wasn't just that it was clean—it was that it was quiet. Not bus-quiet, not exhaustion-quiet. The kind of quiet where your nervous system didn't have to stay on duty.

The kind of quiet that made her ribs suspicious.

Mara tossed her bag onto her bed. "Behold. Civilization."

Riley fell backward onto her mattress. "This feels illegal."

Mara lay beside her dramatically. "Let's never leave."

Which lasted all of sixteen minutes.

A group text went off:

Sloan: Meet in lobby. Mandatory. Industry gauntlet. Wear armor.

Mara groaned into a pillow. "Why are we meeting with suits on our day off? Why do they exist?"

"Because art must suffer," Riley said.

And because someone always wanted to be photographed near it.

They returned downstairs where the band was already looking trapped. Label people buzzed around them like flies around an open soda can. Jax signed something on a clipboard that he definitely did not read. Asher was cornered by a publicist pitching a pre-tour documentary idea that sounded suspiciously like exploitation. Drew kept smiling politely while someone explained NFTs to him, and Rowan seemed close to self-immolation.

Riley caught the phrase "brand narrative" and wanted to fake a fire alarm.

The whole scene had a rhythm Riley recognized from backstage: everyone pretending it was casual while the real negotiations happened in the subtext. Compliments that were actually tests. Questions that were really traps. Smiles that were really contracts.

Theo spotted Riley and visibly relaxed.

Like the room had stopped tilting for half a second.

But then it happened.

The ribs.

Just one pulse.

Soft. Precise. Focused toward—

She turned.

A man stood at the far side of the lobby.

Not management.

Not label.

Not PR.

Not hotel staff.

He wore a blazer too clean for the heat, hair slicked back like he'd been styled for a courtroom. His posture was wrong—not awkward, but intentional. His hands stayed at his sides. His gaze scanned rooms, doorways, people.

Noticing too much.

Missing nothing.

Like security, except without the uniform. Like authority, except without permission.

He didn't fit the lobby ecosystem. Everyone else was performing. He was simply... present. Like a camera that didn't blink.

When his eyes found Riley, they didn't widen or flick or shift.

They settled.

Like he had expected her.

Like she was the appointment.

Riley's ribs buzzed again, sharper.

Theo stepped closer, following her gaze. "Who's that?"

"I... don't know."

Except she did.

Not his identity.

Not his name.

But the hum under her ribs recognized him before her brain did.

Watcher.

Not the Handler—different energy entirely.

Connected.

Waiting.

The Handler was a voice. This man was paperwork.

Mara followed their line of sight. "Oh no. Absolutely not. That man looks like a forensic tax audit in human form."

Taj joined them. "Which one?"

Riley nodded subtly.

Taj's jaw tightened. "Stranger?"

"Yes."

"Following?"

"I don't know."

Taj didn't answer. He just moved—quiet, controlled—toward the man.

The man didn't flinch.

Didn't run.

Didn't pretend to be checking his phone.

He simply stepped backward into the revolving door...

and vanished onto the street.

The revolving door spun like a closing iris. A neat exit. A professional exit. The kind of exit that said: I did what I came to do. I saw what I needed to see.

He didn't look back.

Taj glanced back, concerned. "He knew I was coming."

Riley felt the cold in her bones again.

Broadway roared beyond the windows, neon and honky-tonks and tourists screaming off-key country hits. The city was loud. Alive. Chaotic.

But somehow, impossibly—

It felt like someone had opened a door inside the noise

and let the darkness step through.

And it didn't need the dark to hide here. Nashville hid things in plain sight.

Mara squeezed Riley's wrist. "Stay next to me. This whole city is a red flag wearing cowboy boots."

Theo's voice dipped low. "We'll keep you safe."

Riley nodded.

But her ribs buzzed again
and she couldn't shake the feeling—
Nashville wasn't safer.
Nashville wasn't respite.
Nashville was where the threat wanted them.
Wanted her.
Where the machine had more hands.
More places to disappear.
The Handler hadn't made a move yet.
The other stalker had gone quiet.
Which meant they weren't gone.
They were preparing.
Broadway screamed with laughter outside.
Inside the hotel lobby, Riley felt the first tremor of what the next forty-eight hours would become.
Someone wasn't done with her yet.
And Nashville?
Nashville was the perfect hunting ground.
Because in Nashville, everybody watched the stage—so nobody watched the rig.

CHAPTER ELEVEN
What Even Is Rest

Riley woke up to the sound of Broadway trying to punch through double-paned glass.

Not music, exactly. Not one clean song. A messy layered roar: bass from a bar three blocks away, somebody yelling in the street like they were fighting their own reflection, the occasional squeal-laugh of tourists discovering consequences in real time. Nashville didn't sleep; it just changed shifts.

Nashville didn't rest, either. It just swapped out the playlist and kept grinding its teeth.

For a second she didn't know where she was. The ceiling was too high. The sheets were too soft. The faint smell of eucalyptus and corporate lies drifted through the air vents.

Not a bus.

Hotel.

Right.

Nashville.

Her ribs buzzed once in a sleepy, low register.

Not a siren. Just a you're still in it, congrats.

Like her skeleton had subscribed to a service she didn't remember signing up for.

Across the room, Mara lay starfished on her bed, hair everywhere, one arm flung dramatically over her face like a painting of "Woman Experiencing Too Much."

Riley stared at the ceiling.

"Question," she said finally, voice raspy.

Mara groaned. "No."

"What do people actually do on a real day off?" Riley asked. "Normal people. Not us. Normal people."

Mara peeled one eye open. "You're assuming those exist."

"Just... hypothetically." Riley turned her head. "If you removed tours, load-ins, call sheets, and the constant threat of death, what do humans do when they're not working?"

Mara considered, then rolled onto her side.

"They sleep," she said. "They do laundry they put away the same day. They go to brunch with friends they don't secretly want to strangle. They buy throw pillows. They wander Target for four hours, have an existential crisis in the storage bin aisle, cry in the parking lot, decide to change their lives, then go home and change nothing."

Riley blinked. "That's... dark."

"That's Tuesday," Mara said. "Also they have affairs, join gyms they never use, and pretend meal prepping will fix the hole in their souls."

"I don't think I like this thought experiment anymore," Riley said.

"Welcome to rest," Mara replied. "It's just anxiety with nicer lighting."

Riley thought about the bus bunk—ugly, cramped, familiar. It had never promised peace. This hotel did. That was the difference. That was why it felt like a trap.

Taj knocked at 9:00 a.m. sharp like the world's most serious alarm clock.

"Briefing," he called through the door. "Ten minutes. Conference room three on eight."

Mara rolled off the bed with a noise like a dying animal. "If this is a surprise spin class, I'm burning the building down."

Riley dragged on jeans and a hoodie, shoved her feet into sneakers, and tried not to look at her phone. The unknown text thread from the night before sat there like a landmine.

NICE REFLEXES.
CITY LOOKS GOOD ON YOU.

It had come in not long after yesterday's lobby—after the revolving door, after Taj moved, after Riley had done the hardest thing and stayed put.

She shoved the screen into her pocket instead.

Her ribs buzzed in agreement. Avoidance was a short-term fix. He loved short-term fixes.

He loved anything that made her react. Even silence. Especially silence.

The hallway felt overdesigned – too quiet, too padded, like it expected people to behave. Other crew members emerged in various states of consciousness: some with wet hair, some with hotel coffee, some with the hollow-eyed look of people who'd dreamed about bus bunks and woken up in a mattress they didn't trust.

Riley clocked how they moved now—closer together, less wandering, fewer headphones. The tour had learned, the way animals learned, after a near miss.

Conference room three on eight had been turned into Command Central.

Sloan stood at the head of the table with her clipboard, Ruiz beside her. A Bridgestone security liaison sat stiffly in a polo with the arena logo. Taj took a position by the door, arms crossed.

Even the conference room looked staged for professionalism—water pitchers, notepads, neutral art—like a place built for people to say "just circling back" and ruin someone's week.

Riley chose a chair with sightlines to the door and the hall beyond it without thinking. She hated that "without thinking" had become the problem.

Riley and Mara slipped into seats near the middle. Theo, Jax, Rowan, Asher, and

Drew straggled in seconds later, still soft-edged from soap and sleep.

"Morning," Sloan said, voice all sharp edges. "Here's today. Day off number two was supposed to be free form. It is no longer free form. Congratulations, you've been upgraded to supervised captivity."

Rowan raised a hand. "Do we get a brochure?"

"No," Sloan said. "You get rules."

She ticked them off—not on her fingers, just verbally, rapid-fire.

"No one leaves this hotel alone. No side quests. No sneaking out to see friends who 'just happen to be in town.' If you go to the gym, you tell Taj. If you go to the lobby, you tell Taj. If you breathe funny, you tell Taj."

Taj didn't deny it.

"The buses are staying locked at Bridgestone," Sloan continued. "We've increased overnight security there. All RFID records are being pulled. House security has eyes on every entrance."

Mara murmured, "Except the entrances that mysteriously stop being entrances when someone wants in."

Ruiz took over, voice calm but carrying. "I had the hotel pull system logs," she said. "Keycard activity, service dashboards, internal consoles. Someone accessed your floor's backend overnight from an account that shouldn't be active."

Riley felt a chill skate along her spine. "What did they do?"

"Not much," Ruiz said. "Which is the point. They didn't need to order anything or break anything. They needed to touch something they shouldn't be able to touch and leave without a footprint."

Riley felt that word in her teeth—active. Like a thing could be turned off and stay off. Like the past was obedient.

Asher leaned back in his chair. "So... like a ghost login?"

Sloan shot him a look. He sank lower in his chair.

The Bridgestone liaison offered, tight and unconvincing, "Sometimes accounts linger. Legacy systems—"

Ruiz's eyes flicked to him. "And sometimes people use what lingers."

She faced the room again. "We are not dismissing small touches. Sabotage doesn't always look like rigging. Sometimes it looks like access tests."

Theo's jaw tightened. "He's poking the cage."

"Exactly," Ruiz said. "He wants to see how fast we notice, how we respond, who we send."

Riley's ribs buzzed.

Response time.

Chicago's blackout came back sharp in her memory—the way the whole building held its breath while the crowd turned terror into content. He was always measuring something: distance, delay, the lag between stimulus and reaction.

Like she was a lab rat and the maze was made of cities.

"Any contact from the number?" Ruiz asked Riley.

Riley hesitated. "A couple texts. After the lobby."

"Can I see it?" Ruiz asked.

Riley slid her the phone, thumbprint unlocking it. Ruiz read the messages once, expression not changing, then forwarded them to herself and handed the phone back.

"I'll run it through," Ruiz said. "Don't answer him. Don't block him. For now, we let him think he's getting a rise."

"That's a choice," Mara said.

"I want him comfortable," Ruiz replied. "Comfortable people make mistakes."

Comfortable people got sloppy. Predators got greedy. Riley clung to that like a handhold.

Sloan exhaled. "Bottom line: you treat this hotel like an extended backstage. Controlled. Observed. No solo missions. No mysteries you keep to yourself because it 'might be nothing.' Nothing is nothing anymore. Clear?"

Everyone nodded.

Even Jax, who usually met conflict with a joke.

It hit Riley then, in a quiet, brutal way: they were all scared. Not just of the falls or the water or the blackout, but of the pattern. Of the idea that their lives were becoming someone else's hobby.

Her ribs buzzed once more, faint and furious.

She was too.

Anger sat under the fear now, hot and steady. Fear made you run. Anger made you memorize.

Technically, they were "off" after the briefing.

In practice, no one knew how to be.

Crew wandered the halls like ghosts, drifting between rooms with hotel robes and snacks. Some holed up in the makeshift "crew lounge" conference room, watching terrible daytime TV with the volume low. Others retreated to their own beds with laptop screens glowing blue against tired faces.

Theo knocked on their door mid-morning.

Mara opened it. "If this is a social call, I'm not emotionally prepared."

"It's a practical call," he said. "We're going upstairs. Rooftop."

Mara narrowed her eyes. "You hate rooftops."

"I hate crowds," Theo said. "This is fenced, elevated, and technically optional. It'll do."

He looked at Riley. "You coming?"

Riley hesitated. "Is Ruiz going to yell at us for leaving the floor?"

"She approved it," he said. "Taj is bringing a comm. Also a gun. Also his personality."

"That's a lot of firepower," Mara said.

"Exactly," Theo replied.

The rooftop pool turned out to be closed for the season — tarp pulled tight across the water, chairs stacked and zip-tied like the hotel didn't trust anyone not to try something stupid.

Which, honestly, felt personal.

The space was still open, though. A wide deck overlooking downtown. Concrete warm where the sun hit it, cold where the wind cut through. Spring trying to be convincing without quite committing.

Broadway roared below, softened by height but still constant.

A few other hotel guests lingered anyway: a couple drinking coffee out of paper cups, a guy in a suit pacing with his phone, a woman wrapped in a cardigan taking skyline photos like the weather might change its mind.

Riley watched the suited guy too long.

He looked normal.

That meant nothing. Normal had been retired for a year, apparently.

Taj claimed a spot near the access door, sunglasses on, radio clipped to his belt.

He didn't look like security.

He looked like consequence.

"I'm not getting anywhere near covered water," Mara announced, dropping into a lounge chair and pulling her jacket tighter. "That's how people die."

"It's closed. Not cursed," Riley said.

"You say that," Mara replied. "But I've been on too many tours to believe hazards stay where they belong."

Riley sat on the low concrete edge near the covered pool, hands braced behind her, feeling the sun warm her through her jacket.

Theo sat beside her, sneakers planted, jacket zipped halfway like he couldn't decide whether he trusted the temperature.

"You're not even pretending this is relaxing," she said.

He glanced at the wrapped pool. "I relax when I can see all the exits."

"Fair," she said.

They sat like that for a while — sun in their faces, wind sharp enough to remind them it wasn't summer yet.

For a few minutes, Riley's ribs were quiet.

The quiet made her suspicious.

It also made her want to cry. She hated that too.

She almost forgot about rigging charts and tampered valves and mirrors that wrote back.

Almost.

"What would you do," she asked Theo suddenly, "if you had an actual day off? Like, real one. No shows, no label, no scheduled suffering. Just... nothing."

He thought about it longer than she expected.

"Sleep," he said. "Then make coffee. Then maybe write something that isn't for anyone."

"That's it?" she asked.

"That's everything," he said.

Mara, stretched out behind them with her jacket over her face like a corpse at a spa, added,

"And then spiral about your career, stalk your exes' Instagrams, google your symptoms, and fall asleep on the couch with Netflix asking if you're still watching."

Theo made a face. "Thank you for ruining my fantasy."

"You're welcome," Mara said. "Grounding is my gift."

Riley laughed.

The sound surprised her.

It surprised Theo too. He looked at her like laughter was a rare animal and he was relieved it still existed.

Her ribs buzzed — not in warning this time, but in a strange, aching echo of gratitude.

Like her body was trying to remember what it felt like to be a person instead of an alarm system.

For a second, the world felt almost—
Whole.

The first weird thing happened just after noon.

They came back from the roof chilled and hungry, spring sun having almost fooled them — pink edging Theo's nose, Mara complaining about windburn like it was a personal attack.

The moment Riley opened their hotel room door, the hair on the back of her neck stood up.

Nothing looked wrong at first glance.

Beds: unmade, thank God. They'd slapped the "Do Not Disturb" sign on the outside that morning because neither of them trusted strangers around their stuff.
Lights: off.
Plant lineup on the windowsill: unchanged.
Tilda and her fake siblings stood exactly where they'd left them.

Mara walked in, tossed her tote on the chair, and froze.

"Riley," she said. "Did you leave that there?"

"What?" Riley asked.

Mara pointed at the desk.

A room service tray waited there, gleaming silver domes covering plates they hadn't ordered.

Riley's stomach dropped.

"We didn't—" she began.

"Stay in the doorway," Taj said from behind them.

She hadn't even heard him follow them in.

He stepped past, checked the room with a quick, practiced sweep—bathroom, closet, behind the curtains—then approached the tray.

The check gave him no cover. His shoulders went rigid.

"It's from downstairs," he said. "Real order. Real plates. Problem is, nobody put it on this room."

The sentence hung there, unfinished. Like the only logical ending was: Somebody did.

He lifted one of the domes.

Underneath, on a white plate, someone had arranged the food into a symbol.

Not letters.
Not words.

Slices of strawberries, a bent strip of bacon, two pieces of toast cut into sharp angles.

Together, they formed a shape Riley recognized immediately.

The broken music note.

Her fingers went numb.

Her ribs buzzed like they'd been struck with a hammer.

"Okay," Mara said, voice edged. "That's new."

Theo, who'd been hovering in the hallway, stepped in far enough to see. His face went white.

"Don't touch it," Ruiz's voice snapped from the doorway.

Riley jumped. "How do you keep doing that?"

"Detective privilege," Ruiz said, already pulling gloves from her pocket. "Also Taj called me the second he saw the tray on the cameras."

She crossed the room, studied the plate for a long moment, then lifted her eyes to Riley.

"It's the same shape?" she asked.

"Yeah," Riley whispered. "Lexington. The charm."

"And your dad's case files," Ruiz said quietly.

Riley swallowed hard. "He used to doodle it in margins. Said it helped him think."

Theo looked between them. "Why a broken note?"

"Nobody ever got a coherent answer out of him," Ruiz said. "He said it was how he saw patterns. Things that should fit but don't."

Riley remembered her dad's pen tapping—tap, tap, pause—like he was listening for something under the noise. She'd thought it was a quirk. Now it felt like a warning.

Ruiz took a photo, then another from above, then bagged each piece of food separately like it was evidence in a crime show.

"Who sent that up?" Taj asked.

"Hotel says it was a mix-up," Ruiz replied. "Order was supposed to go to a different room. Ticket got edited in the system and rerouted."

"Of course it did," Mara muttered.

Riley stared at the empty plate now that the pieces were gone. Round. White. Harmless.

Her ribs still buzzed.

"He's in the building," she said.

Ruiz nodded once. "He was before you got here. He's just getting bolder about saying hello."

Bold wasn't the word that scared Riley. Comfortable was.

The day dragged and sprinted at the same time.

Every normal hotel activity felt suspect.

When the fire alarm blipped once at 3:00 p.m. and then went silent, half the crew flinched like they'd been hit. Front desk insisted it was a "panel issue." Ruiz didn't look convinced.

An ice machine down the hall started making a sound like a dying animal, then cut off entirely. Facilities claimed it was old. Mara claimed it was demonic.

Housekeeping knocked twice even with the "Do Not Disturb" sign clearly hanging. The second time, no one was in the hall when Taj opened the door.

Riley's ribs stayed in a low, constant hum.

Not loud enough to panic. Just loud enough to keep her from ever fully exhaling.

By late afternoon, she found herself in the crew conference room again, staring blankly at a muted rerun of Diners, Drive-Ins and Dives while a couple of techs argued quietly about whether Guy Fieri was an agent of chaos or joy.

She didn't register the chair sliding back beside her until Ruiz sat down.

"You look like your brain's buffering," Ruiz said.

"I'm just..." Riley struggled for the word. "Full."

Ruiz nodded. "Understandable."

They watched Guy Fieri bite into something fried and unholy.

"Today was supposed to be rest," Riley groaned.

"This is as close as you get," Ruiz replied. "Rest inside the blast radius."

Riley huffed a laugh. "You are terrible at comfort."

"I'm not here for comfort," Ruiz said. "I'm here to build a case. Comfort is a side effect at best."

Riley glanced at her. "Do you think he's going to hit the hotel? Like, actually do something here? Or is this all just... prelude."

Ruiz considered. "Hotels are messy," she said. "Cameras, witness density, variables he doesn't control. The arena is his playground. This"—she gestured to the room—"is rehearsal space. Access testing. Message delivery."

"The room service thing," Riley said.

"And the little system touches we keep finding," Ruiz replied. "He wants you to know two things: he can reach you when you feel safe. And he's not in a hurry."

"That second one sounds worse," Riley said.

"It is," Ruiz said.

Riley stared at the TV.

"Why me?" she whispered.

Ruiz didn't answer immediately.

"Some people," she said finally, "see patterns. Some people hear them. Some people... feel them. Your father chased his. You notice yours."

"My ribs do," Riley said.

"Same thing," Ruiz said. "He's interested because you're not ignoring the signs like everyone else has. He thinks he can recruit you to his point of view."

"Newsflash," Riley said. "He's doing a terrible job."

"He's not actually trying yet," Ruiz said. "This is him flirting."

Riley made a face. "That's gross."

"Correct," Ruiz said.

Ruiz's calm made it scarier. Like she'd already accepted how bad "trying" could get.

The second weird thing happened that night.

It wasn't dramatic.

No blackout. No fire alarm. No screaming.

Just an elevator.

They'd gone down to the lobby after dinner to steal ten minutes of Starbucks and watch Broadway from behind glass like a nature documentary.

On the way back up, it was just Riley, Theo, and Mara in the car. Taj had taken the stairs with a security guy to "stretch his legs" in a way that made Riley think of large predators patrolling territory.

The elevator doors closed.

The car jerked slightly.

They began to move.

And then the lights blinked out.

Not all the way.

The overheads dimmed to a faint emergency glow. The floor indicator cut off completely. The hum of motion stopped.

They were just—hanging.

Suspended between floors.

Riley's ribs flared.

"Oh absolutely not," Mara said into the shadows. "If this is some hostile hotel version of Saw, I'm suing."

Theo's hand found the rail. "Everyone okay?"

"I'm fine," Riley lied.

Mara slid closer until Riley could feel her shoulder. "You better be, because if I die in an elevator in Nashville I'm haunting this city forever."

The emergency intercom crackled to life.

"Uh, we're having a slight... issue with the panel," a voice said. "Elevator two, we see you're between nine and ten. Just stay calm. We'll get you back moving in a second."

Riley's ribs buzzed harder.

"Ask them how long," she whispered.

Theo leaned toward the speaker. "Timeline?"

"Just a few minutes," the voice said. "We have to reset the—"

The speaker cut out.

A new voice slipped into the tiny space between them.

Not over the intercom.

Not out loud.

Straight through Riley's radio.

She froze.

The unit was clipped to her waistband –
she hadn't turned it off after the briefing,
just muted enough to forget it was there.

"Between floors," the Handler said,
conversational. "Interesting place to stop.
No doors. No exits. Just a box."

The words didn't echo. They didn't need
to. They lived inside her.

Riley's heart slammed. The radio
buzzed faintly on her hip, a small, cold
weight she suddenly couldn't ignore.

She'd left it on channel four.

The private one.

Her thumb twitched.

Theo noticed her shift. "Riley?" he said.
"What?"

She raised a finger. Wait.

Her ribs roared.

"You're good at staying put," the voice
murmured. "Good at not chasing. Good at
noticing without handing yourself over."

Her stomach turned.

"You're good at stairs," he continued, like he was tasting the words. "Always taking side routes. Always knowing where the exits are. But there are places where exits don't matter. Machines break. Cables snap. Gravity wins."

Riley pictured the cable above the elevator car—thin, braided, obedient—until it wasn't.

Her chest tightened. "What do you want?" she whispered, so quietly Mara couldn't catch it. She turned her face slightly away, pretending to be staring at the ceiling.

"What I wanted from your father," he said. "Witness."

"I am not your audience," she said.

"Oh, you are," he replied mildly. "They run because of numbers. Tickets. Streams. Insurance constructs. Attention. You know the machine. You're inside it now. You can feel where it fails before it does. That's... interesting."

The elevator shuddered. Something clanged far above them.

"Leave the tour," he said, voice a soft pressure in her ear. "Go home. Play civilian. Let it happen to someone else. I won't follow you."

"You're lying," she said.

"Of course," he said. "But I like to give people outs. It makes staying feel like a choice."

Like he was generous. Like he wasn't the one tightening the box around her.

The elevator lurched.

Started moving again.

Lights brightened.

Floor indicator flicked back to life: 9... 10...

"Sorry about that, folks," the building voice came back, cheerful and oblivious. "We're back in business. Enjoy your evening."

The doors slid open on nine.

Taj stood there, hand already on the rail outside, as if he'd been prepared to pry it open himself.

"You alright?" he demanded.

"We got stuck," Mara said. "Elevator tried to kill us. It failed. I'm suing."

Theo stepped out, eyes going straight to Riley's face.

Whatever he saw there made his shoulders tighten.

"Riley." Taj said. "Did he talk to you?"

She realized then that her hand was still on her comm, fingers white-knuckled around plastic.

She nodded once.

Taj's expression went flat. Dangerous. "What did he say?"

"He offered me an out," Riley said. "Again."

"New terms?" Ruiz's voice asked from down the hall.

She was walking toward them already, heels silent on carpet.

"Same bargain," Riley said. "Leave the tour, he leaves me alone. Stay, and I'm... useful."

Ruiz stopped very close, gaze sharp. "What did you say?"

Riley swallowed.

"I told him he's a liar," she said. "And that I'm not his audience."

Theo's hand hovered near her shoulder, not quite touching, like he wasn't sure which would break first—her or him.

"Good," Ruiz said. "You keep telling him that. Every time. He thinks your father failed because the machine was bigger. He's expecting you to crumble the same way."

"I'm not my dad," Riley said.

"No," Ruiz agreed. "You have better friends."

Riley felt that in her chest like a bruise you were grateful for—proof something had taken a hit for you.

Mara sniffed. "I'm going to cry," she said. "Out of spite."

That night, Riley lay awake in the dark a while.

Mara's breathing evened out slowly across the room. The glow of Broadway seeped in around the edges of the curtains, painting faint moving lines across the ceiling.

Her phone buzzed once.

She rolled over and squinted at the screen.

UNKNOWN:

GOOD INSTINCTS.

TOMORROW WE PLAY FOR REAL.

Her ribs flared in one sustained note, low and angry.

She didn't answer.

She dropped the phone facedown, pressed her hand over her sternum, and let the buzz rattle her bones until it faded.

She imagined the Handler somewhere in the same city—another room, another hallway, another panel—smiling like he'd just set a metronome and was waiting for her to match it.

Tomorrow was load-in.

Tomorrow she'd walk every inch of Bridgestone with Sloan and Mara and Taj and Ruiz breathing down the venue's neck.

Tomorrow the Handler would have everything he needed.

Height.

Weight.

Crowd.

Rig.

Systems he'd been mapping since Lexington.

Tonight, he'd just wanted to hear how fast her heart beat in a breaking elevator.

Riley closed her eyes.

"Tomorrow," she whispered into the dark, "I'm watching you too."

Her ribs buzzed once, fierce and sharp.

Not fear.

Not warning.

Agreement.

Nashville wasn't done with them.

And neither was she.

In the dark, the city's noise kept going—endless, hungry, bright. Riley let it wash over her like stage wash, like cover, like camouflage.

If the Handler wanted a performance, fine. Tomorrow she'd give him one.

But it wouldn't be the one he expected.

CHAPTER TWELVE
The First Strike

Riley didn't sleep.

Not really.

She drifted, maybe, in the abstract sense — body in bed, eyes closed — but her mind stayed locked in a loop of the Handler's symbol burning across the Broadway billboard. Every time she blinked, the lines rearranged themselves behind her eyelids like a puzzle working backward.

Like the city itself was chewing the shape and spitting it back, over and over, until it stopped being a symbol and became a language.

It wasn't even a nightmare in the normal way. Nightmares had arcs. Nightmares had monsters that jumped out at you like they respected pacing.

This was worse.

This was the feeling of a hand hovering over a light switch for hours. Not flipping it. Not leaving. Just waiting until "dark" started feeling normal.

By sunrise, she felt hungover on fear.

Across the room, Mara groaned into her pillow without lifting her head. "Stop pacing," she mumbled. "You're making my anxiety motion-sick."

"I'm not pacing," Riley lied.

Mara rolled one eye open. "You're doing laps in your mind. It counts."

The hotel room looked like a crime scene made out of comfort. Clean sheets. Thick curtains. Too many pillows. A thermostat that clicked obediently when you touched it, like it hadn't heard of tragedy.
Like it believed "safe" was just a setting, not a lie.

The city outside, meanwhile, was already awake and drunk on itself. Broadway didn't sleep; it just rotated costumes. Overnight neon became morning neon. The same honky-tonk signs, the same bachelorette herds, the same street musicians auditioning for a label that would chew them up and sell their ribs back to them as "merch."

Nashville took everything and renamed it. Pain became *grind*. Fear became *edge*. Survival became *hustle*.

Riley stared at the window until she realized she was holding her breath like the glass might crack if she exhaled wrong.

Her ribs buzzed once—low, private, irritatingly steady. Not a warning siren. A reminder.

Still in it, congrats.

Mara sat up and rubbed her face with both hands like she was trying to wipe the week off. "Okay," she said, voice rough. "We're going to do something radical today."

Riley blinked. "Work?"

"Worse," Mara said. "We're going to act normal."

Riley snorted a laugh that came out thin.

Mara pointed at her. "No. I mean it. We don't let him steal our entire personality. We get dressed, we go to load-in, we do our jobs, we do not spiral in a hotel bathroom. We do not stare at plants like they're informants. We do not become characters in his story."

Riley's ribs buzzed again, like her body had opinions about optimism.

A knock hit the door—two short taps, one long.

Theo's pattern.

Riley froze anyway. Because patterns had started meaning things, and she didn't like that her life was becoming a code.

Mara swung her legs over the bed. "If that's room service arranged into a murder symbol, I'm setting the tray on fire."

Riley opened the door.

Theo stood in the hallway with a coffee that looked untouched and an expression that had chosen calm on purpose. Not soft. Not relaxed. Controlled. Like he'd decided he was the solid thing today and everyone else could orbit him.

"SUV leaves in two," he said.

Riley nodded. "Okay."

His gaze moved over her like a quiet checklist—eyes, hands, posture. He stopped for half a beat at her sternum as if he could hear what she didn't say.

"You eat?" he asked.

"No."

He held the coffee out, then thought better of it and withdrew his hand. "We'll fix it at the arena."

Mara appeared behind Riley, hair in every direction, hoodie shoved on like armor. "If I die today," she announced, "bury me with a laminate and an open bar."

Theo's mouth twitched. "Deal."

They moved.

That was the thing about show day— you didn't get the luxury of falling apart. The schedule didn't care. The machine didn't care. The city didn't care.

And somewhere, Riley suspected, he didn't care either. He just watched.

The SUV ride was quiet in the way a room went quiet after someone said the wrong thing.

Taj rode front passenger, eyes up, chin angled like he was measuring the world for exits. He didn't talk. He didn't scroll. He watched reflections in glass and side mirrors and the faces of pedestrians that turned too slowly. His stillness was a warning label.

Mara slumped against the window, chewing the inside of her cheek like it was a coping mechanism.

Theo sat beside Riley in the back and kept his knee close to hers—not touching, not claiming. Just there. A boundary you could lean into if you started to tilt.

Riley watched Nashville slide past like a set built for tourists: daylight on brick, murals, signs screaming about live music and hot chicken, crowds already forming in packs like they'd been issued an itinerary for chaos.

The city wore daylight like makeup. Trying to look wholesome over last night's sins.

Her ribs buzzed in short, precise pulses—less like panic, more like direction. Where. Where. Where.

Taj spoke once into his comm, low. "Grid checks confirm no anomalies... yet."

Sloan answered from another vehicle. "Nothing moves today without Ruiz signing off. Nothing."

Theo exhaled through his nose like he wanted to laugh and couldn't afford to.

Mara muttered, "Nashville is where the suits come out of the walls."

Riley's gaze snagged on a billboard for a streaming service and the broken note shape flashed in her head so fast it felt like a blink.

She pressed her fingertips to her sternum. Just to remind herself she was still a person. Not a sensor. Not bait.

Theo noticed the gesture anyway.

"You don't have to do this alone," he said quietly.

Riley didn't look at him. If she did, something in her chest might crack open and spill out.

"I'm not," she said.

Her ribs buzzed like they didn't believe her.

Bridgestone Arena swallowed them the moment they hit the loading dock.

The dock doors didn't open so much as inhale—big steel mouths taking the tour whole: truss, video wall, road cases stamped with labels and tape and tired handwriting. Forklifts screamed in reverse. Cases slammed over seams in the concrete like punctuation. Diesel and metal and old popcorn lived in the air like they'd been here longer than the building.

Above, riggers moved along catwalks with grim competence.

This was Nashville. Nobody here treated gravity lightly.

Gravity didn't care how seriously they took it.

Sloan stood center dock with a headset and a clipboard and the violent energy of someone who'd already fought three fires before breakfast.

"No one touches a motor without my sign-off," she barked into comms. "If you put your hands near a hoist without clearance, I will walk you out myself and you will never work in this town again."

A rigger yelled, "Copy!" in a tone that suggested fear had replaced caffeine.

Riley felt the buzz in her ribs tighten into a single concentrated thread.

Not panic. Not yet.

Attention.

Ruiz waited near stage left like she belonged there—hands gloved, posture quiet, eyes taking inventory. She didn't look like a cop visiting a venue. She looked like evidence with a heartbeat.

"Morning," Mara said as they approached, which was generous.

Ruiz's gaze flicked to Riley. "How's your built-in alarm system?"

"Loud," Riley admitted.

"Good," Ruiz said. "Loud keeps you alive."

It wasn't comfort. Ruiz didn't do comfort. She did truth.

Taj stayed near them, scanning. Not fidgeting. Not chatting. Watching the corners. Watching the doors. Watching the places a person could appear if they wanted to.

Show day made everyone move faster.

Show day also made the predators show up.

Backstage, the corridors filled with bodies that weren't crew—people in polos, people in heels, people with lanyards and smiles and the kind of eyes that calculated value. They didn't know the weight of a truss, but they knew exactly what a headline was worth.

The kind of predators who didn't need a knife. Just access.

Riley hated them on principle. This week, she hated them with purpose.

Theo drifted past, guitar case slung over his shoulder. He didn't look at the suits. He looked for Riley, found her, and his shoulders loosened by a fraction like her presence was the only thing that wasn't performative.

"You good?" he asked, quiet.

"No," Riley said.

"Cool," he replied. "Same."

They were running out of words that meant anything.

The dressing room was the only place they could pretend to control.

Riley and Mara went to work on the room the way they always did – lights softened, corners claimed, the air made tolerable. The humidifier hummed quietly in the corner. Plants were repositioned with the seriousness of ritual. Snack appeared in neat rows on the sideboard: fuel, comfort, plausible deniability.

Drew set Tilda the plant dead center on the coffee table like an altar. "This is your light now," he told it solemnly.

Rowan tuned a guitar with his head down like he could build peace out of strings.

Asher ate the gummy vitamins out of sheer defiance.

Jax opened the mini-fridge and yelled, "Why is there only one Red Bull? I feel targeted."

Mara didn't look up. "Maybe the universe has taste."

Theo lingered in the doorway watching Riley work the way he watched the stage— quiet, attentive, trying not to interfere, trying not to miss anything.

"You didn't sleep," he said.

"No."

He nodded once like he'd already suspected. Like he'd been counting the dark circles under her eyes and didn't want to name them.

"If something feels off," he said, "you tell me."

"I will."

She meant it. She was done trying to be brave alone in her own body.

Outside the door, the corridor filled with the constant hiss of show-day movement: assistants running, managers arguing, someone laughing too loudly because that's what fear sounded like in a suit.

Riley's ribs buzzed again—short, sharp.

Ruiz appeared in the doorway.

"We found a mark," she said.

Everything in Riley went cold.

"Where?" Mara asked.

"Loading dock stairwell," Ruiz replied. "Chalk. Thin. Faint. But deliberate."

"His?" Theo asked, voice low.

Ruiz nodded once. "He wants you to know he's here."

Sloan paced two sharp steps like she wanted to fight the building. "Great," she snapped. "Fantastic. I love surprise guests."

Ruiz's gaze didn't move from Riley. "Did you feel it?"

Riley swallowed. "Yeah."

Ruiz didn't look surprised. That was the worst part. She treated Riley like a sensor the tour hadn't known it had until the lights went out.

Being believed didn't feel good when what you were believed about was a monster.

"Show day," Ruiz said quietly, to all of them. "He picked it on purpose. Audience. Cameras. Noise. Confusion."

Mara's mouth twisted. "He's a theater kid."

Theo's jaw clenched. "Can we sweep it for prints?"

Ruiz's eyes stayed flat. "Chalk doesn't love fingerprints. He knows that."

Sloan's voice turned razor-thin. "So what now?"

Ruiz answered without blinking. "Now we assume he's already inside the machine."

Riley's ribs buzzed once—small, furious agreement.

Soundcheck ran quiet.

Suspiciously quiet.

That was always the danger zone. The calm that invited you to believe you had time. Normal was camouflage now.

Riley stood stage left with her clipboard and her headset, eyes sweeping: truss points, safeties, catwalk movement, cable runs. She tracked the band's positions the way a lifeguard tracked swimmers—because any one wrong motion could become a body.

The rig overhead looked perfect on paper. Clean on the plot. Hundreds of pounds suspended by math and trust and the fact that people had decided gravity was negotiable as long as you filed the paperwork.

Her ribs buzzed. A thread tightening.

She looked up.

A single spotlight head twitched.

Not in a programmed sweep. Not in an automated reset.

It dipped—just a fraction.

Like it was looking.

At her.

Her heartbeat stuttered.

Mara appeared at her shoulder. "What."

"The light moved," Riley whispered.

"Lights move," Mara said automatically.

"No," Riley said. "It looked."

Sloan's voice snapped over comms. "Freeze. Ruiz—stage left. Now."

Ruiz arrived, eyes tracking Riley's gaze to the fixture.

The light hung still now. Innocent. Perfect.

Ruiz's jaw tightened. "I want that unit checked top to bottom before doors. Every screw photographed. Every mount tested. I want logs pulled from the board. Twice."

A lighting tech hurried in, hands raised like surrender. "We didn't queue that."

"I know," Ruiz said.

Riley's ribs buzzed again—an echo. A satisfied hum.

Theo walked over mid-soundcheck, guitar still strapped on. He didn't ask. He looked at her face, then at the rig, then back.

He rested his hand lightly at the back of her arm—barely a touch, just enough to anchor her.

"Stay here," he murmured.

"I am here," Riley whispered.

"You know what I mean," he said. Then softer, like it hurt him: "Don't go hunting."

Her ribs didn't care about his logic. Her ribs were tuned to the building, and the building felt like a throat clearing before it spoke.

Doors opened at seven.

Nashville poured in like the arena owed them something—boots, glitter, denim, bachelorette packs moving like swarms. The temperature changed the moment the crowd arrived. The air got wetter, hotter, electric. The building woke up.

Phones rose like offerings. The noise became a living thing.

Riley's dread didn't ease.

It sharpened.

Backstage, the suits hovered in fresh layers of cologne and confidence. Someone from the label asked Sloan if "everything felt stable."

Sloan stared at him like he'd asked her if fire was polite. "Stable?" she repeated. "Sure. Like an oil rig."

He laughed because he thought it was banter.

It wasn't.

Rowan caught Riley for a second in a corridor, voice low. "You feel it."

"Feel what," she asked, even though she knew.

He tapped his chest. "The weight. Like thunder before it breaks."

Riley's ribs answered with a deep thrumming pulse.

"Yeah," she said. "I feel it."

Rowan nodded once, like it was a prayer. "Stay close."

Riley hated the way they were starting to say it. Like she was a charm. Like she was a warning.

Lucky charms didn't end up in evidence bags.

Lucky charms didn't get voicemails from strangers who locked motel doors behind them.

Lucky charms didn't carry panic in their bones.

Theo passed her on his way toward stage, eyes locking on her in a quick check— Are you still here? Are you still you?

Riley lifted her shoulder in the smallest version of yes.

Her ribs buzzed anyway.

The building was waiting.

And so was he.

The show launched like a rocket.

Song One hit and the crowd erupted. Light cut through haze in clean blades. The band moved as one organism, practiced violence made beautiful. Everything worked the way it was supposed to.

For a few minutes, it almost felt like music again.

Like the machine existed to turn noise into joy and sell it back to people as salvation.

Then Song Two started.

And Riley's ribs hit like a fist.

Not a buzz. A jolt. Hard enough to steal her breath.

She scanned fast—deck, wings, grid, the edges where disaster began.

Nothing falling.

Nothing obvious.

Then she saw the pyro tech at his panel.

He wasn't touching anything.

A status light blinked anyway.

ARMED.

His eyes went wide. He jerked his hands back like the console had bitten him and mouthed, "That's not me."

Riley's voice tore out over comms. "CUT PYRO. NOW. DO NOT FIRE."

The panel chirped—sweet, obedient— like it had heard her.

Then a cue executed anyway.

Not the full planned effect.

A short, ugly burst—mis-timed and wrong—spitting sparks out of sequence near stage right.

Asher flinched mid-run and ducked on instinct as the spray hissed past the edge of his lane and scorched the padding behind a speaker stack.

For half a second, the crowd screamed like it was part of the show.

Backstage knew better.

Ruiz grabbed the pyro chief by the vest. "Kill main power."

The breaker dropped. The panel went dark.

The band kept playing because they had been trained to play through panic. To smile through near-death. To make the machine look smooth because the machine paid their rent.

Riley stood frozen, hand clamped over her sternum, ribs screaming, watching thin smoke curl from the wrong place.

It wasn't an accident.

It wasn't a malfunction.

It was a message delivered through heat and timing.

He'd reached a system that could kill someone in a blink.

And he'd chosen not to.

Not yet.

Just enough to prove he could.

Theo turned on the thrust, eyes finding her in the wing. He couldn't hear the voice in her headset. But he could read her face.

Whatever he saw there scared him more than the sparks.

Between lines, he shifted just enough toward stage left to be close without breaking the show.

"Riley," he said, tight. "Look at me."

She forced her gaze to him.

"You're here," he said. "Stay here."

"I'm here," she whispered.

"You know what I mean," Theo said, and it sounded like a plea disguised as an order. "Don't go hunting."

Because hunting meant chasing the dark.

Because hunting meant becoming what he wanted her to be.

Riley swallowed. Her ribs buzzed like an animal trapped in a cage.

She hated that he was right.

She hated that the Handler wanted her to run toward the danger.

She hated that some stubborn, furious part of her wanted to anyway—because running toward it felt like choosing the direction, even if the choice was a lie.

The music surged. The crowd screamed, blissfully unaware they were cheering through a murder attempt.

Backstage, the aftermath moved in tight, brutal bursts.

The pyro tech's hands shook as he slapped safeties on like prayer.

Sloan hit the wing like a storm made human. "Who touched it?" she shouted, not at a person—at the universe. "Who thought this was funny?"

"No one touched it," the pyro chief said, voice thin. "We were dead. Then we were live. The panel—"

"I don't care about your panel," Sloan snapped. "I care about the fact that my band didn't get lit up like a Christmas tree, and I'd like to keep it that way."

Ruiz moved fast, already asking for time stamps, power logs, camera coverage. The kind of evidence that existed in theory and vanished in practice.

Riley stayed at stage left because her legs didn't understand they were allowed to collapse. She kept scanning the rig like staring hard enough could keep it honest.

Her ribs buzzed in sharp stabs, then settled into a low hum.

Satisfied.

Not because it was over.

Because it had worked.

Tonight wasn't the kill.

It was a tap on the glass.

A warning shot dressed up as a cue.

A reminder that the machine could be made to misbehave on command.

Riley pressed her palm hard to her sternum like she could hold her bones still.

She couldn't.

Somewhere inside Bridgestone, something had learned where the switches were.

And it had started practicing.

CHAPTER THIRTEEN
Pattern Recognition

The crowd left happy.

That was the worst part.

They poured out of Bridgestone flushed and hoarse and glowing, phones full of footage they'd rewatch tomorrow with the smug certainty that they'd been part of something electric. They talked about the lights, the encore, the way the band "felt locked in tonight." Someone would post about the sparks and call it insane production value. Someone else would swear it had been intentional.

The machine had eaten fear and turned it into joy again.

Backstage, the air felt chewed.

Riley stood where she'd stood for the last twenty minutes of the show, headset still on, clipboard forgotten at her side. Her ribs had stopped screaming, but they hadn't gone quiet. They'd settled into a low, watchful thrum. Like an engine idling too high.

Theo came offstage damp with sweat and adrenaline, guitar handed off to a tech who looked like he might cry if someone spoke too loudly near him. Theo didn't go to catering. Didn't sit. Didn't celebrate.

He went straight to Riley.

"You okay?" he asked, voice careful. Not loud enough to draw attention. Not soft enough to be meaningless.

Riley nodded once. Then again, smaller. "Nobody got hurt."

"That wasn't the question," he said.

She exhaled through her nose. "I'm still upright."

Theo held her gaze for a beat, then nodded like that was enough for now. It wasn't relief. It was triage.

Behind them, Sloan was already dismantling someone with her voice.

"I do not care how many redundancies you think you have," Sloan snapped at the pyro chief. "If a system arms itself without human input, it is no longer a system. It is a liability."

Ruiz stood with her, arms crossed, eyes sharp, listening without interrupting. She didn't need to raise her voice. She just needed people to understand she was writing things down in her head that would follow them forever.

Taj hovered at the edge of it all, scanning. Always scanning. The crowd was gone, but the building wasn't empty yet. Venues had long memories and too many places to hide.

Mara appeared at Riley's side, shoved a bottle of water into her hand. "Drink," she said. "Before you forget how."

Riley obeyed automatically.

"Congrats," Mara continued. "We survived Nashville Night One without dying. That means statistically Night Two is a nightmare."

"Please don't say things like that," Riley muttered.

Mara shrugged. "If I don't joke, I scream."

Riley almost smiled.

The debrief happened in a windowless room that felt temporary by design.

Of course it did.

The band sat slouched and damp, adrenaline bleeding out of them in slow waves. Crew packed in along the walls. Everyone looked tired in that hollow, wired way that came after a near miss you weren't allowed to acknowledge in public.

Ruiz stood at the front with her jacket off and her sleeves rolled like she was about to scrub in.

"Let's be clear," she said. "What happened tonight was not a malfunction."

No one argued.

"The pyro system armed without command input," she continued. "That means someone accessed either the panel software or the power routing. We're pulling logs, but I'm telling you now—this wasn't a guy with a grudge and a wrench. This was someone who knew what to touch and when."

Sloan crossed her arms. "Meaning?"

"Meaning he didn't want casualties," Ruiz said. "He wanted reaction."

Riley's ribs buzzed once, sharp agreement.

"He wanted to see how fast we'd notice," Ruiz went on. "How fast we'd shut it down. Who moved first."

Taj spoke up from the corner. "He got data."

"Yes," Ruiz said. "And he left satisfied."

That landed harder than if she'd said danger.

Theo leaned forward, elbows on his knees. "So what's the play tomorrow?"

Ruiz met his eyes. "Tomorrow, we assume he'll push further. Different system. Different timing. Same goal."

"Which is?" Asher asked.

Ruiz didn't answer right away.

"To see if Riley breaks," Mara said flatly.

The room went still.

Riley felt every head turn toward her, even the ones trying not to. She hated that she didn't feel embarrassed. She hated that it felt... accurate.

Ruiz nodded once. "Yes. And to see who breaks with her."

Theo's jaw tightened.

Riley swallowed. "I'm not—"

"I know," Ruiz cut in gently. "This isn't about blame. This is about reality."

Sloan exhaled hard. "So what do we do?"

Ruiz's gaze slid back to Riley. "We stop pretending he's just a voice. He's operational now."

Riley's ribs buzzed again, low and steady.

Operational.

That was the word.

The hotel room felt smaller when they got back.

Not physically. Psychologically. Like the walls had leaned in while they were gone.

Mara kicked off her boots and collapsed onto the bed face-first. "If anyone needs me, I'll be dissociating into the mattress."

Riley set her clipboard down with care, not remembering when she decided to. She moved like she was underwater, every motion delayed.

She peeled off her hoodie and sat on the edge of the bed, staring at her hands. They looked normal. Steady. Like they hadn't just watched a system decide whether to kill someone.

Her phone buzzed.

Once.

She froze.

Mara lifted her head an inch. "If that's him, I'm throwing your phone out the window."

Riley glanced at the screen.

UNKNOWN.

No message preview. Just the name, sitting there like a dare.

Her ribs flared—not panic. Anticipation.

She didn't answer.

The phone buzzed again.

UNKNOWN:

CLEAN RECOVERY.

Riley's stomach turned.

UNKNOWN:

YOU SHUT IT DOWN FAST.

She dropped the phone onto the bed like it burned.

Mara sat up fully now. "Okay. Nope. Absolutely not. What did it say?"

Riley swallowed. "He's... grading us."

Mara stared at her. "I hate him."

"Good," Riley said. "So do I."

The phone buzzed again.

UNKNOWN:

TOMORROW IS DIFFERENT.

Riley picked it up this time before Mara could object.

Her thumbs hovered over the screen.

Mara's voice was quiet. "You don't have to answer."

"I know," Riley said.

Her ribs buzzed—short, insistent.

She typed.

RILEY:

No one died.

The reply came immediately.

UNKNOWN:

THAT WAS THE POINT.

Her hands went cold.

UNKNOWN:

YOU FELT IT BEFORE IT HAPPENED.

Riley's chest tightened.

UNKNOWN:

THAT MAKES YOU RARE.

She stared at the words until they blurred.

UNKNOWN:
SLEEP. YOU'LL NEED IT.

The typing bubble vanished.

Silence rushed back in like it had been waiting.

Mara reached over and took the phone from Riley's hands without asking. Set it face down on the nightstand. "He doesn't get to tuck you in."

Riley let her.

Sleep didn't come easily.

Riley lay in the dark listening to the building settle, the distant echo of Broadway still bleeding through the night. Every sound registered as potential. Every silence felt loaded.

Her ribs buzzed intermittently, like a reminder alarm she couldn't disable.

She thought about the pyro console arming itself. About how close the sparks had come. About how the crowd had screamed like it was part of the show.

About how easily danger became spectacle.

About how the Handler hadn't needed to touch anything with his hands.

He'd touched the system.

And systems didn't feel pain.

She rolled onto her side, staring at the faint glow leaking around the curtains.

Tomorrow was Night Two.

Same building. Same crowd. Same machine.

But now it knew her.

And worse—

She was starting to understand it.

Her ribs buzzed once more, deep and resonant.

Not fear.

Recognition.

And somewhere in Nashville, a man who never showed his face was already planning the next test, confident that she'd feel it coming.

Confident she wouldn't look away.

Riley closed her eyes and let the noise of the city cover her like static.

If he wanted an audience—

Fine.

But she was done being passive.

Tomorrow, she wouldn't just react.
Tomorrow, she'd listen back.

CHAPTER FOURTEEN
Teeth

Nashville woke up wrong.

Not storm-wrong.

Not omen-wrong.

Wrong in a way Riley felt before she even opened her eyes — a quiet, pressing heaviness in the air, like the city itself was bracing. Like someone had pulled all the oxygen out of the day and forgotten to put it back.

Like a held breath stretched too long. Like anticipation without hope.

Her ribs buzzed low and steady.

Not warning.

Prediction.

The kind of certainty that didn't ask permission.

Mara sat at the little hotel table eating cereal straight from the box like a raccoon in designer sweatpants. "Well, you're making your haunted face," she said. "What's the vibe? Ghosts? Stress ulcer? Death?"

"All of those," Riley said.

"That's Thursday," Mara replied. "Get in the car."

Security had doubled overnight. Taj looked like a man who hadn't blinked since the blackout. Two extra SUVs flanked theirs as the convoy pulled away from Broadway. Sloan sat in the front passenger seat speaking rapid-fire orders into two different phones.

The kind of multitasking that came from knowing failure would be very loud and very public.

Theo slid into the seat beside Riley looking more awake than should've been legal.

"You good?" he asked.

"No," she said.

He nodded. "Me neither."

The honesty landed heavier than reassurance.

Mara glanced at them. "Oh great. My two most dramatic coworkers are synchronized today."

Taj muttered, "Stay alert. Ruiz flagged new intel."

Riley's ribs buzzed hard enough to make her grip the seat.

"What intel?" she asked.

Sloan turned slightly in her seat. "Symbols."

"Plural?" Riley said.

Ruiz's voice crackled over the radio. "Three more. One on the perimeter fence. One under the loading ramp. One chalked in a dressing-room hallway at five a.m."

Riley swallowed. "He's marking the building."

"He's laying in territory," Ruiz corrected. "This show isn't random. He wants this one."

Like a predator circling before the bite.

Theo stiffened beside her. "Why Nashville?"

Riley already knew the answer.

"Because tonight has the biggest spotlight," she said quietly. "And he loves spotlights."

And because Nashville knew how to look away.

Load-in moved with surgical precision — the kind that only comes when everyone is terrified and pretending not to be. Crew snapped to orders faster than Sloan could give them. Every rigger checked every point. Twice. No one touched Pyro without Ruiz watching.

Fear made excellent employees.

Riley walked the floor.

The ribs stayed on constant buzz mode, a steady pulse beneath her sternum, like a metronome set just too fast.

Like the song was already playing, just out of human hearing.

Theo approached with his guitar in hand. "You feel it already?" he asked.

"Yes."

"Strong?"

"Too."

He exhaled. "Tell me if it spikes."

"I always do," she said.

He hesitated. "You didn't always."

"That was before it almost killed the drummer," Riley said. "We're past my rebellious phase."

Past denial. Past pretending instincts were optional.

A voice behind them muttered, "Hey!" Drew was holding Tilda the plant like a protective father.

"She thrives on chaos," he said.

Mara side-eyed him. "She needs therapy."

So did all of them.

At 5 p.m., Sloan dragged everyone into a conference room overlooking the bowl. Band. Crew chiefs. Ruiz. Taj. Riley. Mara.

Sloan closed the door with the ceremony of a funeral.

"Tonight's show," she said, "is not optional. The label will die before they cancel it."

Rowan raised a hand. "Love the pep talk."

"But," Sloan continued, "we are not pretending nothing is happening. Everyone in this room knows we have an active threat following this tour. Ruiz has confirmed this individual was in the building last night."

A ripple moved through the room — not panic. Recognition.

Theo's jaw locked.

Jax dropped his protein bar.

Asher muttered, "Fantastic."

Sloan pointed at the whiteboard. Ruiz had written one phrase:

THE PATTERN IS ESCALATING.

Riley's ribs buzzed, sharp this time.

Ruiz looked at her. "You feel it now?"

Riley nodded once.

Theo leaned forward. "So what do we do?"

Ruiz answered. "We don't give him easy openings. He wants impact. Visibility. Drama. So we limit his variables."

Sloan pointed at Riley. "Which means she does not move alone tonight."

Riley blinked. "I never move alone.".

Theo turned. "She's with me."

Sloan raised a brow. "Are you volunteering or declaring?"

"Both," he said.

Mara leaned over to Riley. "Aw. He's imprinting."

Riley elbowed her.

Ruiz capped her marker. "He will strike tonight."

A heavy silence dropped.

Riley's ribs buzzed like agreement.

Like her body had already accepted the terms.

The band ran their set list under amber work lights. Riley hovered stage left, but never more than ten feet from Theo. Taj and two additional security officers watched from opposite wings. Ruiz stood at FOH, scanning the grid through binoculars.

Riley hated every second.

The ribs buzzed almost constantly now — not in panic, but in certainty.

Panic wobbled. Certainty locked in.

Theo tuned silently beside her. "He's here," he said quietly.

"Yes."

"Where?"

"I don't know."

Theo's hand brushed hers — just barely — like he was grounding her.

"If it gets bad," he said, "I'm getting you off the deck."

"I'm not leaving the deck," she replied.

"Then I'm staying with you."
Neither of them smiled.

Mara passed them carrying three towels and a bag of cough drops. "Cute. Romance by imminent murder."

Fans poured in, screaming, glittering, chanting song lyrics. The arena pulsed like a living creature, every seat filled, every body buzzing. Nashville crowds were loud in a way that felt personal.
Like they wanted blood or salvation and couldn't tell the difference.

Theo stepped past Riley toward the wings as preshow timers started. "See you on the other side," he said softly.
She didn't let herself say the truth — that she didn't know what "other side" meant anymore.
Survival had stopped feeling linear.

The show started perfect.
Too perfect.

Song One: flawless.
Song Two: electric.
Song Three: Riley's ribs began to ache.

That was new.

A deep inner pressure — like something was clenching her spine.

Like the warning system had shifted from signal to pain.

She scanned the deck.

Nothing wrong.

Grid.

Nothing obvious.

Wings—

Her breath froze.

A man in black stepped through a restricted tunnel.

He wasn't crew.

Wasn't vendor.

Wasn't band-adjacent.

His badge was wrong.

Too shiny.

Too new.

Untouched by sweat. Untested by labor.

And his face—

Riley recognized the *shape* of him.

Not because she'd seen him clearly before.

But because her ribs exploded with a sudden, violent pulse.

The Handler.

She couldn't breathe.
Her body reacted before fear could form words.

He slipped deeper into the tunnel, out of sight.
"Taj!" Riley hissed into her comm. "He's inside. Section C tunnel. Moving upstage."

Theo looked over mid-song — eyes sharp, catching the fear in her face.
Ruiz's voice cut in: "Everyone freeze positions. DO NOT go after him alone."

But Riley was already moving.
Because instincts didn't wait for permission.

She cut behind the last cable trough and into upstage shadow.

The air felt different back here — tighter, charged.
Like the building had inhaled and was waiting.

Her ribs pulled *up*.
Not forward.

Upstage, above the deck, a flown scenic lighting element hovered just out of work-light range — a rectangular steel truss

241

dressed with blinders and effect fixtures.
Part of the visual hit for later in the set.
Normally parked at high trim, locked,
ignored.

It should not have been moving.

The winch whined.

Low.

Controlled.

Active.

Riley froze.

The element was descending.

Slow enough to look intentional.

Fast enough to be deadly.

She looked up.

On the upstage catwalk, silhouetted
against dim service light, stood a figure.

The Handler.

He wasn't looking at her.

He was watching the stage.

Watching Theo step into position.

Like this was timing, not violence.

"HEY!" Riley shouted.

He turned his head.

Half his face stayed in shadow beneath
the wide brim of his hat.

The other half curved into a faint, curious smile.

Not anger.

Not excitement.

Interest.

Below them, FOH rolled low-end into the room — subs waking the building as the next song intro swelled.

The vibration traveled up the steel.

The truss descended another foot.

Too low now.

Too close to the deck.

Riley sprinted to the nearest dead-man stop, slamming her palm into the emergency kill.

Nothing.

The override was locked out.

"FLY COMING IN!" she screamed. "CUT IT—CUT IT NOW!"

Theo looked up.

Time slowed.

Crew shouted.

Radios erupted.

Someone yelled for automation.

The truss kept coming.

Not free-fall.

Worse.

Controlled descent meant to look clean.

"MOVE DOWNSTAGE!" Riley screamed, voice tearing. "NOW!"

The band reacted on muscle memory alone.

Theo yanked Rowan backward.

Asher dove clear of the zone.

Drew dropped off his riser.

Jax scrambled sideways into a monitor stack.

The truss crossed its safe trim.

Steel screamed.

Then the safeties finally caught — shock-loaded, violent — snapping the element sideways as thousands of pounds swung hard and slammed into the deck where Theo had been standing seconds earlier.

The impact thundered through the arena.

Lights shattered.

Metal rang.

The crowd screamed.

Riley looked up.

The catwalk was empty.
The Handler was gone.
He hadn't needed to watch the landing.

Alarms blared — not the dramatic kind, the building kind. The ones that meant protocol, not theater.

House lights bumped up. FOH killed the walk-in music.
The crowd noise didn't drop so much as *change shape*—confusion turning into a wave that didn't know where to land.

Sloan was already on comms. "Hold. Hold. Hold. Freeze the deck."

Security sealed the wings.
Crew swarmed the impact zone with that terrifying calm tour people wear when panic is a luxury item.

Theo grabbed Riley first — hands on her arms, hard enough she could feel the outline of his fingers later.

"You could have died," he choked out.

"So could you!" she shot back, voice shaking with anger because shaking was better than falling apart.

His forehead touched hers, breath uneven. "Stop doing that."

"Doing what?"

"Taking hits meant for us."

His voice cracked on *us* like the word hurt.

Riley didn't know how to answer that. She was still hearing metal scream. Still feeling the moment her body went cold and certain.

Ruiz shoved through the cluster, eyes already scanning, already counting. "He was here. Confirmed sighting?"

Riley nodded once.

Taj looked like he wanted to tear the arena apart with his hands. "We're ending the show."

Sloan snapped, "No. The show goes on."

Theo rounded on her, raw and loud. "THE HELL IT DOES."

Sloan flinched — not from fear, from the fact that it was *Theo*.

Ruiz pinched the bridge of her nose like she was holding a migraine in place. "Everyone calm down. We can still control the narrative."

"What narrative?" Mara barked. "The part where a man tried to drop the rig on us? That narrative??"

Riley was shaking. She didn't try to stop it. Stopping it felt like pretending.

Ruiz stepped close, voice low enough it didn't become content. "Riley. Did he speak again?"

Riley shook her head.

"Did he... acknowledge you?"

Riley hesitated.

Then nodded.

Everything in the wing went quiet — not peaceful, *listening*.

Theo's voice dropped. "What did he do?"

Riley met his eyes.

"He smiled."

It shouldn't have resumed. Not cleanly.

But arenas don't do clean — they do containment.

Automation killed the motors. The flown element was hard out and tagged. Ruiz made the house rigger photograph every point like it might lie under pressure.

A PA announcement went up to the crowd: *brief technical issue, thanks for your patience*—the dry lie that kept twenty thousand people from stampeding toward exits.

Then Sloan made a choice that tasted like iron.

A revised plot. No upstage travel. No scenic moves. No fancy hits. Everything tightened down to the safest version of itself.

The crowd roared when the band came back, because applause is what people do when they don't know what else to do with fear.

But the energy was different now.

Desperate.

Raw.

Too awake.

The band played like their lives depended on it.

Theo kept glancing stage left where Riley stood.

Riley kept scanning the tunnels and catwalk lines and the dead spaces cameras never loved.

Her ribs buzzed nonstop — not panic, not warning. A steady count.

The Handler didn't reappear.

He didn't have to.

Tonight wasn't about killing them.

It was about showing her the truth:

He could reach any part of the machine. Any credential. Any override. Any door that "shouldn't" open.

He wasn't in her comm. He wasn't stalking from a distance.

He was here — inside the building, inside the heartbeat of the tour, inside the lie that safety could be enforced if everyone just followed the rules hard enough.

When the final chord hit, the arena shook like it was trying to pretend nothing had happened.

Theo didn't even take off his guitar before he ran to her.

He pulled her into a crushing hug that felt more like *proof* than comfort.

"You cannot," he whispered into her hair, "ever run into the dark alone again."

Riley didn't argue.

Couldn't.

Mara crashed into them next. "I swear to God, Kentucky, if you die before I do, I'm haunting you."

Ruiz approached slowly, expression set. "We need to talk in private."

Taj stepped between them. "Not tonight."

"Yes," Ruiz said — gentle, which somehow made it worse. "Tonight."

Riley looked at all of them:

Theo.

Mara.

Rowan hovering like he didn't trust his own lungs.

Asher pacing.

Drew hugging Tilda like she could anchor reality.

Taj's fury.

Sloan's collapse held upright by sheer will.

Ruiz's grim certainty.

Her ribs buzzed one last time.

Not a warning.

A promise.

This wasn't over.

This was the beginning of the war.

CHAPTER FIFTEEN
The Watcher

The hardest part wasn't the crash.
It was the applause after.
Because Nashville clapped like they'd just watched a stunt. Like the scream that tore through the bowl was a sound effect. Like the metal that hit the deck and dented it was set dressing. Like Theo yanking Rowan out of the impact zone was choreography.

They clapped because the lights came back.
Because the band kept moving.
Because people will cheer anything if you don't let them see the ambulance.

Backstage, the world was quieter—but not calmer.

Quiet was just what happened when everyone had agreed, without speaking, that panic would make it worse.

Riley stood in the wing and watched crew swarm the fallen platform like ants around a dropped sugar cube. The smell of hot metal and dust and something electrical hung in the air. Someone had unplugged something they shouldn't have, then plugged it back in like that fixed the fact that a man had just tried to kill a band live in front of twenty thousand screaming fans.

Her ribs were still buzzing.

Not screaming now.

Shivering.

Like a live wire after the breaker flips.

Residual danger. Residual rage.

Theo stayed near her like a shadow with a heartbeat.

He didn't touch her—except once, briefly, when a stagehand rolled a road case too close and Theo's hand landed on Riley's shoulder like an automatic safety. A reflex. A warning. A promise.

Mara hovered on Riley's other side with a towel in one hand and the expression of a woman who wanted to bite a wall.

"Okay," Mara whispered, voice too bright, "I am officially adding 'falling platforms' to my list of reasons I hate men."

Riley stared at the dent in the deck. "You're running out of paper."

"I'll get a notebook," Mara said. "A binder. A three-ring. An encyclopedia."

Sloan was pacing a trench into the concrete.

That was what she did when she couldn't scream.

Or when she was saving the scream for someone with a job title.

Ruiz moved through it all like she had her own gravity—gloved hands, eyes scanning, phone up, already snapping photos of bolts and mount points and the rack Riley had body-checked like she was made of insurance claims.

Taj stood by the upstage tunnel with two security guys and a face that said: *If I catch him, it won't be a lawful arrest. It'll be a lesson.*

"Private," Ruiz said, and it wasn't a suggestion.

Riley's throat went tight.

Theo's hand flexed at his side like he wanted to say no on her behalf.

Ruiz clocked it. "Not you, Theo."

Theo's jaw ticked. "She's not going alone."

Ruiz didn't blink. "She's not. Taj can stand outside the door and glare at drywall."

Taj's voice was flat. "Happy to."

Mara lifted a finger. "I'm also attending. I'm the emotional support animal."

Ruiz looked at Mara. Looked at Riley. Exhaled like a woman who'd stopped fighting inevitability somewhere around Cincinnati.

"Fine," Ruiz said. "But if you interrupt me once, I'm cuffing you to a chair."

Mara held up both hands. "I love consequences. Proceed."

The production office at Bridgestone was pure utility.

Folding tables shoved together. Power strips spidering across the floor. Radios charging in mismatched rows. Clipboards stacked like they might topple if someone breathed wrong.

Empty coffee cups crowded every flat surface – evidence of decisions made too early and revised too late.

A whiteboard leaned against the wall instead of being mounted, its schedule already smudged where someone had wiped it down and written over it again.

It felt obscene that the room existed at all.

That after what had almost happened, there were still spreadsheets.

Ruiz shut the door.

The quiet inside hit hard.

Not peaceful.

Soundproofed.

Taj took his post by the door like a statue with a pulse. Theo leaned against the far wall, arms crossed, gaze on Riley like he was trying to keep her here through force of attention.

Sloan didn't sit. She paced once. Stopped. Stared at Ruiz.

"Talk," Sloan said.

Ruiz set her evidence bag on the table. Inside it, a piece of chalk sat sealed like it was radioactive. Next to it: a photo printout of the symbol from the loading dock stairwell. And another. And another.

Three symbols. Three locations.
A triangle around the building.

A map drawn by a man who liked being seen.

"He was in the arena before doors," Ruiz said. "We have footage of someone in black moving through the service corridor at 6:12. Face obscured. Hat. Badge visible long enough to confirm: fake laminate."

Riley's stomach turned.

"Because of course," Mara muttered. "He's craftsy."

Ruiz ignored her. "He didn't enter through the main dock. He didn't enter through a public door. He's in the back end of the building. Places only staff go. Which means—"

"Access," Sloan snapped.

"—someone let him," Ruiz finished.

The room went colder.

Theo's head lifted. "You think it's an inside job?"

Ruiz's eyes flicked to him. "I think it's either inside help, or he's good enough to make it look like inside help."

"That is... not comforting," Mara said.

"Nothing about this is for comfort," Ruiz replied.

Riley's ribs buzzed—sharp, irritated—like her body hated the word *inside*.

Because *inside* meant the tour.
Inside meant the machine.
Inside meant: someone had been smiling at them while holding the door.

Sloan planted both hands on the table. "We need to shut this down. Tomorrow. Tonight. Cancel the next city. Cancel the whole leg."

Ruiz's expression didn't change, but her voice tightened a fraction. "You can't cancel your way out of a pattern."

"Oh," Mara said. "That's a fun sentence. Love that for us."

Ruiz slid a folder across the table toward Riley.

It was old.
Worn at the edges.
Not an arena document. Not a tour doc.
A case file.
Riley's breath caught as she saw the name.

Her father.

Her dad's handwriting in the margins. The same looping pen strokes she'd seen in childhood grocery lists and sticky notes on the fridge.

Her ribs flared like they recognized the ink.

Ruiz watched her reaction without flinching.

"You told me he doodled it," Ruiz said quietly. "The broken note. In his margins."

Riley swallowed. "He did."

Ruiz opened the folder to a page Riley had never seen.

A photo. Grainy. Black-and-white.

A symbol chalked on a concrete wall. Slightly smeared. Same shape. Same broken note.

Under it, in her dad's handwriting:

STAGE ACCESS. NOT RANDOM. HE WANTS WITNESS.

Riley's throat went tight. "What is this?"

Ruiz's voice dropped lower. "A cold case your father worked. Twelve years ago. Three incidents. Different venues. No deaths, but close calls. Always near-load, near-fall, near-fire. Always in public. Always with plausible deniability."

Theo's face went still. "He did this before."

Ruiz nodded once. "And your father thought the person responsible wasn't after bodies."

Sloan spat the word like poison. "Then what?"

Ruiz's gaze held Riley's. "After belief."

Riley's ribs buzzed like a chord struck too hard.

Mara's voice came soft for once. "Riley…"

Riley couldn't look away from the file.

Her father's handwriting stared back like a ghost with a badge.

"I didn't know," Riley whispered.

Ruiz didn't soften. "You were a kid. He kept it from you. Probably because he wanted you safe."

"And he failed," Riley said.

Theo's head snapped toward her. "Hey."

Riley blinked hard. "No. He—he died chasing something he couldn't prove. And now this man is doing it again. And he's—"

She swallowed. "He keeps bringing my dad into it like he has a right."

Ruiz's voice sharpened. "He's doing it because it gets under your skin."

"It works," Riley said. "Congratulations to him."

Mara let out a shaky breath. "So we're in a sequel."

Sloan's laugh was bitter. "We're in a franchise."

Ruiz flipped to another page.

A list of names.

Not victims. Not suspects.

Witnesses.

People her dad had interviewed. People who'd been near the incidents.

One name was circled in thick pen:

WATTS, E.
(SECURITY / CONTRACT) — REFUSED FORMAL STATEMENT

Riley's ribs buzzed, quick and sharp.

"What?" Ruiz asked instantly.

Riley stared at the circled name like it had teeth. "Watts."

Riley frowned. "Like... Taj?"

Taj's head turned from the door. For the first time in the room, his expression shifted. Not fear. Not anger.

Recognition.

Mara's voice rose an octave. "Oh my God. If this turns into betrayal, I'm flipping a table."

Taj stepped forward slowly, controlled. "My last name isn't Watts."

Ruiz didn't blink. "I know."

She tapped the file.

"E. Watts," she said. "Not you."

Taj's gaze narrowed. "Then why is that name hitting you like that?"

Riley swallowed. "Because... because I saw someone today."

Everyone stilled.

Sloan's eyes sharpened. "The lobby guy."

Riley nodded.

"The man in the blazer," Riley said. "The one who looked like he didn't belong. He left when Taj approached. He... he looked like he expected me."

Ruiz's jaw tightened. "Describe him."

Riley tried. Slick hair. Clean blazer. Wrong posture. Camera eyes.

"He didn't feel like the Handler," Riley said. "But he felt... connected. Like—like a second hand on the same clock."

Ruiz pulled out her phone. Swiped. Turned the screen toward Riley.

A photo.

Old. Slightly blurred.

A man on a sidewalk outside a venue— half-profile, blazer, slick hair, a badge clipped wrong.

"You mean him?"

Riley's ribs went nuclear.

Her vision tunneled for a second.

"Yes," she whispered. "That's him."

Theo's voice was quiet but edged. "Who is that?"

Ruiz's eyes were hard. "That's Elias Watts."

Mara made a sound that was half laugh, half choke. "Elias is such a villain name."

Sloan's voice went ice-cold. "And who the hell is Elias Watts?"

Ruiz didn't break eye contact with Riley. "He worked event security on the same circuit your father was investigating. He was present at two of the incidents. He refused a statement. He disappeared before your father could subpoena him."

Riley's mouth went dry. "And now he's here."

Ruiz nodded. "Now he's here."

Theo pushed off the wall, one step closer to Riley like he was going to physically block history from touching her.

"What does he want?" Theo asked.

Ruiz's answer was quiet. "I don't know yet."

Riley's ribs buzzed in furious agreement.

Because she did know the shape of it.

Not the motive. Not the plan.

But the pattern.

A Handler who loved the show.
A Watcher who loved the ledger.

One to push the machine.
One to measure the fallout.

"Okay," Mara said, voice shaking with anger she was trying to joke around. "So we have The Handler and... The Accountant."

Ruiz didn't smile. "We have two moving pieces now."

Sloan exhaled, sharp. "So what's the move?"

Ruiz folded her hands on the table like a judge. "We stop treating this like a single offender."

Theo's voice was tight. "And Riley?"

Ruiz looked at Riley again. "Riley is still the best early warning system we have."

Riley flinched. "I'm not a—"

"A thing ," Ruiz finished, softer than usual. "I know. You're a person. Which is why I'm telling you this now: your instincts are useful, but they are not a leash he gets to hold."

Riley's ribs buzzed hard.

Because that was the thing.

He kept trying to make her chase. Trying to make her witness.

Ruiz leaned in slightly. "He smiled at you because you did exactly what he wanted."

Riley's stomach turned.

Theo's voice went rough. "She saved us."

Ruiz didn't deny it. "And he watched her do it."

Sloan slapped a hand on the table. "So we shut down every access point. We triple security. We—"

Ruiz cut her off. "We do that, yes."

Then, quieter:

"But we also stop reacting like he's the only one steering this."

Taj's voice was low. "Watts is the one feeding him routes."

Ruiz nodded once. "Or feeding him timing."

Mara's eyes narrowed. "Or feeding him rooms."

Riley's ribs buzzed at the memory of the room service tray. The elevator. The internal phone spoof.

Everything that felt like someone knew the building better than a stranger should.

Ruiz slid one more paper across the table.

A printed screenshot from a hotel system log.

A room service ticket with a timestamp.

Not their room number.

But routed to theirs.

A reroute. A click. A change.

Ruiz tapped the paper once. "This was done from a staff terminal."

Sloan's mouth went hard. "So it's inside. Again."

Ruiz's gaze sharpened. "Or it's Watts using inside."

Theo's hands curled into fists.

Riley's ribs didn't buzz now.

They went still.

Not calm.

Focused.

Because in the stillness, a thought settled cleanly in her brain like a key turning:

This wasn't just about killing them.

It was about turning the tour into a demonstration.

A lecture.

A show within a show.

And she was the one he kept trying to put onstage.

"No emergency moves," she said. "No sudden changes. We don't give him the satisfaction of disruption."

Sloan frowned. "So what do we do?"

Ruiz's gaze stayed on Riley. "We keep going."

Taj nodded, already reaching for his radio. "Copy. Tour continues"

Theo's gaze held Riley's. "You're not doing this alone."

Not a question.

Riley's ribs buzzed once—soft, stubborn, accepting.

Mara sighed like a woman exhausted by destiny. "Of course we aren't stopping. That would be boring."

Ruiz's phone buzzed.

She checked it.

Her expression changed—not fear. Not surprise.

Annoyance.

Which was somehow worse.

"Ruiz?" Sloan demanded.

Ruiz turned the phone so they could see the screen.

A single text.

Unknown number.

NICE RECOVERY.

NEXT TIME, PICK FAST.

YOU CAN'T SAVE BOTH.

Riley's ribs lit up like a match.

Theo swore under his breath.

Mara whispered, "Oh, I hate him. I hate him so much."

Ruiz stared at the message for one extra beat. Then she looked at Riley.

"Congratulations," Ruiz said quietly. "He just changed the game."

Riley swallowed. "How?"

Ruiz's voice stayed calm, which meant it was serious.

"Because until now," she said, "he was proving he could reach you."

She held up the phone.

"Now he's proving he can force you to choose."

Riley's ribs buzzed—low, furious, relentless.

And somewhere, deep under the noise of the arena and the noise of Nashville and the noise of fear, Riley realized something that tasted like iron:

The Handler didn't want her dead.

He wanted her responsible.

He wanted her to carry the weight of every near-miss like a confession.

He wanted her to become what her father became—

A person who lived inside the pattern until the pattern lived inside him.

Riley looked at Theo. At Mara. At Taj. At Sloan. At Ruiz.

Then she said the only true thing in the room:

"Not this time."

Her ribs buzzed once.

Not warning.

Not prediction.

Decision.

CHAPTER SIXTEEN
The Spin

The worst part was how fast the building forgot.

Bridgestone didn't linger in shock. It didn't hold space for almost. It did what arenas were built to do: reset. Sweep. Power cycle. Flip the lights. Move on. The machine didn't have the luxury of trauma, and it didn't grant it to anyone else.

Riley sat on a folded road case in a service hallway and watched normality get rebuilt around the absence of catastrophe.

Barricades went back into place.
Cables were re-coiled.
A dented rail was measured, photographed, and quietly taped off like a bad memory.

A stagehand pushed a broom past a scrape in the deck without slowing.
A lighting tech rolled a cart of spare fixtures around the impact zone like the platform hadn't almost rewritten someone's life.
Two venue managers argued in low voices

about insurance language and liability thresholds.

Nobody said *almost*.

Nobody said *dead*.

Nobody said Theo's name out loud in the sentence Riley kept replaying anyway.

Seconds earlier.

Her ribs had finally stopped buzzing long enough for something worse to arrive.

Aftermath.

It sat heavier. Slower. Less dramatic. It didn't scream. It settled. Her hands shook with the delayed insult of it, like her body resented being useful before it was ready.

Mara crouched in front of her, elbows on her knees, eyes too steady.

"You're doing the thousand-yard stare again," Mara said.

"I'm thinking," Riley said.

"That's the stare you get right before you do something brave or catastrophic," Mara replied. "So I'm going to hover."

"I'm not doing anything," Riley lied.

Mara's mouth twitched. "That sounded like a vow made at speed. Not binding."

Across the hallway, Sloan was on her third war.

You could tell by the way her voice flattened—emotion stripped out, replaced with something sharper and more durable.

"No," Sloan said into her phone. "You don't get to cancel. You weren't here. You don't get to discover ethics because a clip crossed your desk."

A thin voice crackled back.

Sloan closed her eyes. Opened them. "Do not say 'brand risk' to me while I'm standing in steel-toed boots next to a broken rail. If you want a hometown moment so badly, you can come hang from the grid yourself."

She ended the call without ceremony.

Then she saw Riley.

Something in Sloan's expression shifted—not softness. Not kindness. Calculation.

"Chase," Sloan said. "Up."

Riley stood because her body still responded to commands even when her brain lagged behind.

Sloan nodded toward production. "Ruiz is in the office. Label wants in. PR is already halfway in. We're deciding what version of tonight survives."

Mara rose too. "Love that for us."

"You're coming," Sloan said. "You bite."

"Correct," Mara replied. "It's my primary skill."

Riley followed them down the corridor. Her ribs didn't buzz. No direction. No warning.

Just a dense, listening quiet.

Like whatever lived under her sternum had gone still to take notes.

The production office looked exactly like it did less than an hour ago. Mara muttered, "I hate when you get sent back to the principal's office twice in the same day. It's never for the same crime."

Ruiz stood over the table, laptop open, venue maps spread out like she was preparing to invade a small country. Sleeves rolled. Gloves gone. All attention forward.

Taj took position by the door.

Not leaning.

Not resting.

Locked.

Theo sat on the edge of a chair, guitar case still strapped to him like muscle memory. His knee bounced. His eyes tracked Riley the moment she entered.

He didn't say her name.

He didn't have to.

Are you still here sat on his face like a question.

Riley nodded once.

Ruiz saw it. Filed it.

Sloan shut the door.

"Ground rules," she said. "We don't panic on record. We don't feed speculation. We don't use the phrase 'attempted murder' anywhere near a phone."

Theo's head snapped up. "That's what it was."

"I know," Sloan said. "This is about containment, not truth."

A PR rep cleared his throat. Young. Polished. Too clean for a room that still hummed with residual danger.

"We're seeing traction," he said carefully. "Clips are already circulating."

Mara's face went flat. "Define traction."

He turned his phone.

A vertical video. Shaky. Loud. The moment of failure slowed, stabilized, annotated by strangers who mistook proximity for expertise.

Caption:

NASHVILLE GOT A SPECIAL EFFECT??

Comments blurred past too fast to read.

Theo looked away first.

Riley didn't.

It wasn't the footage that hit her.

It was the tone.

The way disaster became novelty the second it survived.

Sloan's voice dropped. "We issue a statement. Dry. Boring. Safety-focused."

Theo's laugh scraped. "That's a lie."

"It's a firewall," Sloan said.

Ruiz leaned in. "Words don't change what happened. They change who shows up next."

Mara nodded. "Also TikTok detectives with ring lights."

Ruiz's mouth twitched once.

Taj spoke for the first time. "We also have a leak problem."

Sloan turned. "Explain."

"Clips hit before the band cleared the deck," Taj said. "That's not fans. That's someone inside pushing content."

The room cooled.

Ruiz said quietly, "Watts."

Theo's hands curled. "So he's feeding the crowd."

"Or feeding the Handler," Ruiz replied. "We don't know which direction the data flows yet."

Riley's ribs buzzed—small, irritated.

Because *data* felt wrong in this context.

Too clean a word for blood-adjacent math.

Sloan planted her hands on the table. "Fine. We starve it. We control what we can."

Theo shook his head. "The internet doesn't starve."

Mara added, "It forages."

Ruiz tapped her keyboard. "I want timestamps. Metadata. Posting order. Who amplifies first."

Sloan frowned. "You're profiling."

"I'm mapping," Ruiz said, eyes flicking to Riley.

Riley's ribs buzzed once.

Maps.

Theo leaned forward. "He smiled at her."

Silence.

Riley felt heat crawl up her neck—not fear. Something closer to exposure.

Ruiz didn't look away. "Tell me exactly what you saw."

Riley stared at the legal pad. At the words pretending a platform hadn't almost rewritten the night.

"He wasn't rushed," Riley said. "He wasn't hiding. He was watching."

"Like it was data," Mara said.

Riley nodded.

Theo looked like he wanted to break something solid and didn't know where to aim.

Sloan exhaled. "So what is this?"

Ruiz answered carefully. "This wasn't escalation."

Mara frowned. "It felt like escalation."

"It was a probe," Ruiz said. "He learned who noticed. Who reacted. Who didn't freeze."

Riley's ribs went still.

Not calm.

Aligned.

"He's not trying to collapse the tour," Ruiz continued. "He's testing the system."

Theo's voice went low. "And Riley?"

Ruiz met Riley's eyes. "She's not the target. She's the metric."

The word landed heavy.

Riley didn't flinch.

Because it fit.

The room shifted.

Not panic.

Recalibration.

Sloan nodded slowly. "Then we adjust operations."

Theo shook his head. "You don't adjust people."

Ruiz said, "We protect them while we learn."

Riley found her voice. "If you pull me, he learns something else."

Theo turned to her. "Riley—"

"I know," she said. "But he's not asking if I'm scared. He's asking if I see."

Ruiz watched her closely.

Then nodded.

Her phone buzzed.

She checked it.

Annoyance crossed her face—quick, sharp.

She turned the phone so only the room could see. Same unknown number. Same taunt as earlier—shorter this time, like he expected them to remember.

Theo swore softly.

Mara exhaled through her teeth.

Ruiz locked the phone. "That wasn't a threat."

Sloan frowned. "Then what was it?"

"A confirmation," Ruiz said. "He got the answer he wanted."

Riley's ribs buzzed—steady, controlled.

Not fear.

Calibration.

She met Ruiz's gaze. "Then he's going to keep asking."

Ruiz nodded. "Yes."

Riley looked around the room—at Theo's clenched hands, Mara's razor attention, Taj's quiet readiness, Sloan's brutal competence.

"Good," Riley said.

Theo stared at her. "Good?"

"Yes," she said. "Because now we know what kind of question it is."

Her ribs buzzed once.

Not warning.

Not prediction.

Preparation.

They didn't go back to the hotel the way people imagine recovery happens.

There was no exhale. No safe room. No morning-after clarity.

The tour absorbed Nashville the way it absorbed everything else—by folding it into logistics.

Even two scheduled days off had come and gone without rest.

Security briefings replaced sleep.

Credential audits replaced small talk.

Comms were rebuilt. Channels renamed. Handsets swapped without ceremony. Routes shifted. Not announced. Just done.

Riley learned quickly what the machine did with trauma:

it archived it.

By the time the buses rolled again, Nashville wasn't a crisis—it was a reference point.

A line item.

And whatever had watched her from the shadows didn't disappear during the quiet.

It adjusted.

CHAPTER SEVENTEEN
Calibration

The next show day arrived like nothing had happened.

New city.

New arena.

Same rules pretending to be different.

Riley clocked it the moment they unloaded.

Not wrong.

Not dangerous.

Just... tuned.

Crew moved a half-second earlier than usual.

Security lingered at choke points longer than necessary.

Local hands were polite in that brittle way that meant they'd been warned without being told why.

The machine had tightened.

No announcement. No panic.

Just subtle corrections made by people who knew how close they'd come to a headline.

Riley adjusted her headset and stepped into position stage left.

Different floor. Different paint lines. Same geometry.

That was the part that mattered.

Stages lied about being unique.

They weren't.

They repeated themselves with different lighting.

Theo passed her on the way to soundcheck, guitar slung low, eyes already scanning before the room filled.

"You good?" he asked quietly.

Riley nodded. It was true in the way that mattered.

"I think so."

He didn't ask what that meant.

That was new.

Soundcheck rolled.

FOH ran low-end tests—controlled, professional, nothing like Nashville. Subs came up in clean waves. No rattles. No complaints. No drama.

Riley watched the rig respond.

Every movement logged.

Every correction noted.

She wasn't looking for danger anymore.

She was looking for interest.

Nothing obvious surfaced.

Which didn't relax her.

It sharpened her.

Mara sidled up beside her, arms crossed. "I hate when things behave. It feels sarcastic."

"Give it time," Riley said.

Mara glanced at her. "You're not joking."

"Nope."

House opened.

The crowd poured in like they always did—happy, loud, unaware they were entering a controlled environment designed to feel spontaneous.

Riley watched faces instead of fixtures.

Phones up.

Eyes bright.

No one looking where weight and timing mattered.

The show started clean.

Too clean.

By the third song, Riley felt it—not a buzz, not a warning.

A recognition.

Someone was watching how she watched.

Not following her.

Not interrupting her.

Tracking response time.

Tracking correction patterns.

Tracking what she noticed *before* she spoke.

It wasn't pressure.

It was assessment.

Between songs, Ruiz's voice came through Riley's ear—low, precise.

"Anything?"

Riley paused half a beat longer than protocol.

"No," she said.

Then, after a breath: "But something's taking notes."

Silence on the line.

Then Ruiz: "Copy."

That was all.

Mid-set, Riley caught movement near a secondary access corridor.

Not a threat.

Not even a person who didn't belong.

Just someone who paused when Riley looked.

Who didn't flinch.

Didn't rush.

Didn't pretend.

A man in a jacket.

No badge visible.

No phone raised.

Watching the room like it was data.

Riley didn't move toward him.

She didn't alert security.

She just watched him back.

He left after thirty seconds.

Not chased.

Not confronted.

Logged.

The show ended without incident.

No gasps.

No screams.

No edits going viral before the encore finished.

The crowd left happy.

Which somehow felt worse.

Backstage, the machine reset again.

Load-out started.

Paperwork moved.

People joked too loudly like laughter could cauterize memory.

Sloan called it "a good night" without meaning it.

Ruiz didn't correct her.

Taj walked Riley halfway to the bus, then slowed.

"They're not trying to scare you," he said quietly.

Riley looked at him. "No."

"They're seeing what you do when nothing goes wrong."

"Yes."

Taj nodded once. "That's more dangerous."

On the bus, Riley sat alone for the first time since Nashville.

Not isolated.

Just... unoccupied.

Her phone stayed silent.

No messages.

No threats.

No games.

Which told her everything.

This phase wasn't about forcing choices.

It was about measurement.

About figuring out whether she was useful.

Outside the window, the city blurred into highway, into dark, into the next venue already waiting for them.

Riley leaned her head back against the bus couch, the steady vibration humming through her as she let herself think the thought she hadn't said out loud yet.

They weren't trying to make her the reason.

They were trying to see if she was the kind of person who would stop being one.

Her ribs didn't buzz.

They held steady.

Ready.

Because if this was a test—

She wasn't planning to pass it quietly.

CHAPTER EIGHTEEN
Unresolved

They didn't talk about Nashville.

Not because they were avoiding it. Because everyone already knew which version would surface if they did.

The bus rolled west under a sky that had forgotten stars existed. Curtains half-drawn. Screens dimmed. Conversations reduced to logistics and jokes that didn't land.

Someone snored.
Someone scrolled.
Someone stared at nothing like it might blink first.

Riley lay in her bunk with one arm tucked under her ribs, the other curled around her phone like it might run.

Her body had finally stopped buzzing.

That worried her more than the buzzing ever had.

The absence felt... deliberate.

Like the silence after feedback drops out.

Like a room waiting to hear what you say next.

She checked the comm on instinct.

Dead channel.

Reassigned.

Clean.

Good security.

Good sense.

Still—

She couldn't shake the feeling that something had *noticed* the quiet too.

Above her, the bus hummed with that low, constant motion that usually soothed her. Tonight it felt like being carried somewhere she hadn't agreed to yet.

Mara shifted in the bunk across the aisle. "You asleep?"

"No."

"Same."

Silence stretched between them.

Then Mara said, softer, "You didn't do anything wrong."

Riley didn't answer.

Not because Mara was wrong.
Because the statement didn't fit the shape of what Riley felt.

Wrong implied rules.
This didn't feel like rules.

It felt like observation.

Theo padded down the aisle a minute later, careful, barefoot, hoodie pulled on like armor he could sleep in. He didn't speak at first. Just leaned against the edge of Riley's bunk and let the bus rock them both.

"You okay?" he asked finally.

Riley considered lying.
Considered telling the truth.
Landed somewhere in between.

"I think," she said slowly, "that if I hadn't been there... it still would've happened."

Theo frowned. "What do you mean?"

"I don't think I stopped him," she said. "I think I was part of it."

Theo straightened a fraction. "Part of *what*?"

Riley stared at the ceiling panel, at a hairline crack she hadn't noticed before.

"Not the accident," she said. "The question."

Theo didn't push.

He was learning when not to.

Mara sat up, pulling her blanket around her shoulders. "Okay, I officially hate that sentence."

Riley almost smiled.

Almost.

Her phone vibrated once.

Not a call.

Not a text.

A system notification.

NO SERVICE.

Then—just before the screen went dark—

A preview banner slid down and vanished before she could open it.

Unknown sender.

No message.

Just a timestamp.

Mara leaned over. "What?"

"Nothing," Riley said.

Which was true.

And wasn't.

Theo watched her face instead of the phone. "That was something."

Riley swallowed. "It was... empty."

Theo didn't like that answer.

Neither did she.

The bus hit a patch of rough road.

Everything rattled.

Then smoothed out again.

Riley's ribs stayed quiet.

Not calm.

Alert.

Like whatever lived under her sternum had learned the difference between danger and evaluation.

She lay back, eyes closing, listening to the road, the breathing, the soft human sounds that meant *this part* of the world was still intact.

Just before sleep took her, a thought slipped in — unwanted, uninvited, fully formed:

This wasn't about making her fail.

It was about seeing **how she noticed**.

What she saw.

What she chose to act on.

What she ignored.

What she couldn't look away from.

Her father had seen patterns too.

That hadn't saved him.

But it had made him interesting.

Riley turned onto her side, pulling the blanket up like it could protect her from implications.

Her phone buzzed again.

This time, it stayed.

One line.

No name.

YOU SEE DIFFERENT.

SO DO WE.

Riley didn't reply.

Didn't move.

Didn't wake anyone.

She let the screen go dark on its own and closed her eyes, heart steady, breath controlled, mind racing just enough to be dangerous.

Somewhere between waking and sleep, one last realization settled — heavy, undeniable, impossible to shake:

They weren't trying to turn her into the reason.

They were trying to decide
whether she could be trusted
not to become one.

The bus carried them onward.

And in the dark, Riley understood
something that felt like the beginning of a
war she hadn't volunteered for—

Not everyone who notices the flaw
is meant to stop it.

Some are meant to prove
it exists.

Her ribs stayed quiet.

And that was how she knew
this wasn't over.

CHAPTER NINETEEN
The First Broken Note

Morning didn't announce itself.

It seeped in through the cracks.

A change in the pitch of the road.
A subtle shift in engine rhythm.
Light pressing through curtains that hadn't moved.

Riley woke before the bus stopped.

She always did now.

Her phone lay dark in her hand. No new messages. No service. No proof that all the things she'd seen hadn't been half-dreams stitched together by exhaustion and adrenaline.

But her ribs—

Her ribs remembered.

The bus rolled into the next city under a sky the color of wet concrete. Not hostile. Not kind. Just indifferent. The kind of sky that watched things happen and didn't intervene.

Theo was already up, sitting at the table with a mug of coffee he hadn't touched.

"You good?" he asked.

Riley nodded automatically. Then paused. Corrected herself.

"I'm awake," she said.

Theo accepted that for what it was.

Outside, crew began to unload like nothing had changed. Doors opened. Cases rolled. Radios crackled with familiar voices using familiar language.

Load-in.

Call times.

Coffee runs.

Someone complaining about the dock.

Normal rebuilt itself fast.

Too fast.

Riley stepped off the bus and felt the ground register under her boots—solid, unremarkable, real. The venue loomed ahead, anonymous in the way all arenas were anonymous. Concrete. Steel. Glass. A building that could be anywhere.

That was the problem.

Taj fell into step beside her without comment. Not looming. Not crowding. Just present. A quiet acknowledgment that the rules had changed, even if no one was saying so out loud.

"You're not on deck alone today," he said.

It wasn't a question.
It wasn't an order.

It was policy now.

Riley nodded. "I know."

Inside, the building smelled like nothing yet. No heat. No electricity burn. No crowd.

Just potential.

She paused at the threshold without realizing it.

Theo noticed. "What."

Riley shook her head. "Nothing."

But she was wrong.

She could feel it—the way she always did now. Not a buzz. Not a warning.

A hum.

Like a note played so low most people didn't register it as sound.

She stepped inside.

The day unfolded cleanly. Too clean.

Rigging checked out.

Power was stable.

No loose hardware.

No unexplained delays.

No flickers, no glitches, no bad feelings sharp enough to name.

If someone had been watching for chaos, they would've been disappointed.

Riley walked her routes. Checked sightlines. Logged small things she always logged. A cable dressed tighter than necessary. A badge clipped slightly wrong on a guy she didn't recognize—but when she doubled back, he was gone.

Normal things.

Tour things.

Still—

Her ribs never fully settled.

Midafternoon, Ruiz passed her in a hallway, phone to her ear, eyes sharp. She paused just long enough to meet Riley's gaze.

A look passed between them.

Not reassurance.

Not fear.

Recognition.

That night, the show went off without incident.

No malfunctions.

No near misses.

No screams that weren't part of the set.

The crowd roared. The band played. The lights hit their marks.

Perfect.

After the encore, as the applause swelled and the house lights rose, Riley stood in the wing and felt something hollow out in her chest.

Not relief.

Disappointment.

She didn't like that about herself.

On the bus later, exhaustion hit hard and fast. The kind that shut down thought before it could spiral.

Riley crawled into her bunk and let the curtain fall closed.

Dark.

Quiet.

Motion.

Her phone vibrated once.

This time, she didn't jump.

She opened it.

No number.

No thread.

No history.

Just a photo.

A piece of paper on a table.

White.

Uncreased.

On it, drawn in careful black ink—

A musical note.

Broken clean through the stem.

Underneath it, a caption.

FIRST OBSERVATION COMPLETE.

Riley stared at the screen.

Her ribs didn't buzz.

Didn't flare.

Didn't warn.

They went still.

Not because she was safe.

Because something had decided she was worth continuing.

Riley locked the phone, set it face-down, and lay back as the bus carried them into the dark between cities.

She understood it now—not the system, not the scale, not the money or the machinery behind it—

But the role they were circling.

They didn't want her fear.

They didn't want her obedience.

They didn't even want her silence.

They wanted her *attention*.

Because attention was the rarest thing on a tour built to distract.

Riley closed her eyes.

Sleep came slowly.

And with it, a final thought that didn't comfort her at all:

The most dangerous part of noticing the flaw

was realizing how many people had already seen it—

and decided

to look away.

The bus kept moving.

The note stayed broken.

And somewhere, far beyond this city, the pattern waited

to see what Riley Chase would do next.

END OF BOOK ONE

EPILOGUE

The arena tour ended quietly.

No crashes.

No alarms.

No statements that needed lawyers.

Just buses pulling away from buildings that forgot them the moment the power dropped.

Riley should have felt relief.

Instead, she felt something loosen.

The ribs didn't buzz anymore.

They stayed still.

Waiting wasn't a warning.

It was a condition.

At home, she slept for nearly fourteen hours straight. No dreams. No flashes. Just black.

When she woke, her phone had one new notification.

Not a text.

A calendar update.

SUMMER ROUTE — TENTATIVE

Festival holds.

Multi-day builds.

Temporary structures.

Notes she recognized immediately:
custom steel
expanded grid
redundant load paths
weather contingencies
Bigger stages.
More moving parts.
Less containment.
Festivals didn't remove danger.
They spread it wider.
Riley stared at the screen longer than necessary.
Arenas were controlled machines.
Known ceilings. Known limits.
Festivals were architecture assembled fast, dismantled faster, and trusted to behave under pressure it was never meant to hold.
She locked the phone.
Across the room, her father's notebook sat where she'd left it. Closed. Heavy. Patient.
She didn't open it.
She didn't need to.
Whatever had been watching her hadn't gone away.

It had learned she noticed.
Riley lay back down.
Sleep came.
It just didn't feel like rest anymore.

COMING SOON

Book Two in The Broken Notes Saga

Shadows at Center Stage